NOT FOR ME

THE WINDY CITY CHRONICLES, BOOK ONE

KAT DE FALLA

This is a work of fiction. Names, characters, and incidents are either the product of the author's imagination or used fictitiously, and any resemblance to actual persons living or dead, business establishments, events, locales, is entirely coincidental.

Not for Me

COPYRIGHT © 2018 by Kat de Falla

All rights reserved. No part of this book may be used or reproduced in any manner whatsoever without written permission of the author or SunMoon Arts Publishing except in the case of brief quotations embodied in critical articles or reviews.

Contact information: info@sunmoonarts.com

Cover Art by *Debbie Taylor* © 2018 by DCA Graphics

SunMoon Arts Publishing

Visit us at www.sunmoonarts.com

The Windy City Chronicles

Published in the United States of America

To Lee, who tamed the shrew and plays the lead in my Shakespearean Romance.

CHAPTER ONE

MANDA

*"Sometime all full with feasting on your sight,
And by and by clean starved for a look;"
(Shakespeare Sonnet 75)*

Frigid Saturday morning in late December: Lincoln Park, Chicago

"Our Princess Cupcake book made the *New York Times* Best Sellers list! Now we can add that to the banner for your book signing. You've done it! This is like the fifth message I've left you, Maggie! Please call me back so we can celebrate. I've got the champagne chilling in the fridge for when you get here next weekend!" I hung up the phone and frowned down at the screen, waiting for it to light up with Maggie Monroe's photo. Why wasn't she calling back? This was her baby after all. I was just her literary agent.

But today I was feeling like one hell of a fine agent. I'd managed to take Maggie's dream and help her turn it into a reality. Cupcakes and princesses. That was the idea she'd pitched me in Chicago at the author event before she moved to

Boston. I loved it and signed her within twenty-four hours of our first meeting. Best move of my life. Of course, Maggie wasn't my only client, but she was my first and, secretly, my favorite.

Shoving my phone into the back pocket of my jeans, I tried in vain to rein in my rescue bulldog-lab mix, Beefer, who was successfully dragging me through the polished revolving doors and into the refurbished foyer of my downtown condo. "Heel, Beefer. Heel!" He outweighed me by thirty pounds of pure muscle and, based on his forward lunging, was well aware of the treat awaiting him in the apartment.

The building's doorman, George, paused from sweeping the tile floor. "Slow down there, Manda!" At his full height, he still stood an inch shorter than my meager five foot six. The buttons on his black, double-breasted suit coat squeezed a bit when he bent to pick up a crumpled piece of paper.

I reached down and grabbed it for him. "I got it, George," I said before tossing it in the garbage. His fogged, round glasses and ruddy cheeks implied he'd just stepped in from outside as well. "Thank you. By the way, your dad is keeping me company this fine morning while he waits for you. He *says* he's in no hurry." George gave me a quick wink.

Dad clicked a forefinger on his wristwatch from where he sat waiting in the condo's lobby. The man valued punctuality, a trait I hadn't quite mastered. I gave him a quick wave. "George, stall him for a few more minutes, will you? Beefer and I slept in."

George tipped his hat. "Will do, Miss Wolfgram."

"You're the best." I wondered when people wouldn't require his personalized services and his job would become obsolete, like a lift operator. Could a fingerprint scan, automated key cabinet, computerized voice, or online concierge ever replace George's warm handshake, sports small talk, or friendly face? His capacity for remembering names, faces, and people's schedules was uncanny.

The closest elevator sported an "out of order" sign. The second elevator seemed in permanent halt on the eighth floor. It crossed my mind to take the stairs, but cardio before brunch might turn my stomach. Or so I convinced myself. I let my finger trace the circle of the up arrow button before pressing it, thinking about the poor lift operator. Funny how I lived in a building with hundreds of strangers and it never seemed to bother anyone but me. Everyone was so engrossed in antisocial technology. Always looking down and missing the whole world happening around them. Engaged in electronic conversations when flesh and blood people surrounded them. The modern day domination of parasocial relationships made me sad.

The last guy who'd asked me out checked his phone every five minutes over dinner. Huge red flag. When he'd texted to ask me out again, he received the same stock response I gave to most potential clients and boyfriends, "Sorry, not for me."

The lighted numbers above the elevator marked its snail-like descent to the lobby. Beefer planted his furry backside on the cold tile floor, tail swishing like a restless mop. The high ceiling in the atrium allowed the morning sun to burst through the massive windows where it splashed against the rose-tinged marble floors, making the lobby sparkle like a ballroom. I imagined women with bodice-hugging gowns and full satin skirts curtsying as their partners bowed before sweeping them around the dance floor.

Women should meet men at balls, not bars.

The doors opened, jolting me from my British Renaissance daydream enough to step inside the claustrophobia-inducing metal box. The doors started to close when a series of rapid clicks and heavy footsteps pounded toward the elevator. A deep voice yelled, "Hi ya, George! Hey, can you hold the elevator?"

I knew that voice. *Oh no!*

With a jerk forward, I managed to hit the little button with two outward pointing arrows. A hand appeared in between the doors to stop them from shutting. The doors reopened. My throat seized shut, and time froze.

The sixth-floor hottie!

Every time we passed, I couldn't form a coherent sentence. My brain cells deserted me when his male perfection entered my personal space. The last time we passed in the lobby, it was summer and Beefer sniffed his golden's butt to my utter mortification. I think I mumbled "I'm sorry" and fled in horror.

Today I will form words!

Emboldened, I stood taller and began to formulate a witty question. My cheeks burned while I resisted the urge to gawk. He was bundled up in a winter coat and heavy boots, holding a bag of groceries and wearing an ushanka winter hat that covered most of his face. But it was him. I knew for sure because of the dog.

Instructing myself to take deep breaths, I vowed I'd say something funny and interesting. I was a literary agent for crying out loud! I lived in a world of words. But then I caught a whiff of him: masculine and heavy, like black pepper and tangerines with a splash of the fresh cool, Lake Michigan wind. After that, all words eluded me. Blank. I had nothing.

"Thanks for holding the door." He spoke. *To me.* And in the most polite manner, his hint of a smile melting my insides like hot chocolate after a winter snowball fight.

The elevator slid shut. I stole a sideways glance, and his gray-green eyes locked on mine for a fraction of a second too long.

I jerked my head toward the front of the elevator again, swallowing copious amounts of saliva. *Great, I'm about to drool over this guy for real!*

He reached across and hit the buttons for the sixth and eighth floors. He raised one eyebrow. "Eight, right?"

I nodded like an idiot from my stupor, wishing I could channel chameleon superpowers and melt into the wall.

Hold up! He knows what floor I live on?

Trying to focus on something else, I watched his waggy-tailed golden retriever, who had pranced into the confined space and planted its furry backside right next to its owner.

He pulled a flask from his jacket and unscrewed the cap. After taking a swig, he held the bottle out to me.

I couldn't do anything but give him a confused expression. The elevator stopped at four, but the hall was empty. I risked a look inside his paper bag. A stalk of celery was sticking out next to a nudie magazine. My precious sixth-floor hottie was hot all right…a hot mess.

"So no?" He calmly covered his flask and put it away. "Oh, Desdemona, if only she knew 'I have very poor and unhappy brains for drinking.'" He mumbled the whole thing while patting his dog on the head.

Who the heck was this guy? Quietly quoting Shakespeare but drinking from a flask in an elevator with a girlie magazine in his grocery bag? I mean, where was the guy I saw this summer out for a run? The guy whose T-shirt was sticking to him in all the right places? The guy with the defined shoulders and rippled abs that made me want to ski up and down their slopes?

"What's your name, big guy?"

Beefer puffed out his chest to be macho and sat up nice and tall while the sixth-floor hottie scratched his chin.

"His name is Beefer," I answered, realizing how uncool his name was compared to Othello's Venetian debutante. "Desdemona?" I said it out loud because I still couldn't believe it.

"Nobody gets the reference. No worries."

The elevator opened on the sixth floor, and he stepped out.

"Shakespeare's *Othello*," I said without a moment's hesitation. "I'm…I'm a literary agent."

He turned quickly and stuck his hand in the other pocket of his coat. His eyes brightened, and one corner of his mouth lifted in a half smile as the door began to close. He stuck his arm inside, risking bodily injury, and the door shut on his outstretched hand.

He dropped something.

The door opened all the way back up as a safety precaution, and I bent down to pick up the piece of paper. Now it was my turn to force the elevator into an indecisive pattern. I stuck my head out into the hallway and followed the direction of Desdemona's wagging tail. "Hey, you dropped this."

"It's for you. If you really like Shakespeare, come see me," he stopped walking and looked over his shoulder.

I looked down to find a ticket for *Romeo and Juliet* at Navy Pier for today!

I nodded like a mute fool. My wit and vocal chords were failures and would get a stern admonition later. The mute fool —the only character to cast me as if Shakespeare eviscerated me in fiction.

I stepped back and allowed the door to finally shut. *Did the sixth-floor, day-drinking, girly-mag-reading hottie just ask me on a date?*

Did it matter? He'd basically dropped a free theater ticket in my lap.

An apropos *Othello* quote popped into my head: "Kill me tomorrow, let me live tonight!" I unlocked my apartment, unsnapped Beefer's leash, and filled his water bowl. *Of course, it isn't a date!* After slurping water and dripping it all over my tiny kitchen floor, Beef trotted to the bedroom, jumped up on the bed, and plopped down on his pillow, giving me his look of, "What?"

"I many have to rename you 'Brutus' to up my cool factor." *Not. A. Date.*

Because if it were, I'd have to fess up that I spoon with a dog every night, and unless he sprouts soft, warm fluffiness from every follicle, the dog stayed in the bed. I couldn't get the image out of my mind of the nearly naked girl on the cover of the magazine he'd made no attempt to hide.

The sixth-floor hottie was definitely not for me. But that was no reason not to dress up and go to the theater. No frumpy work clothes for this classy chick.

Yeah, right. Like I could pull that off.

CHAPTER TWO

HARRY

"O! she doth teach the torches to burn bright"
(Romeo and Juliet 1.5.46)

As soon as I opened the door to our apartment, I sniffed in disgust. "Dane," I called out, "this place reeks, and I gave my ticket away to some chick in the elevator." Who'd smelled awesome.

My twin came strolling out of the bathroom in a towel. My brother was every girl's dream hunk. And I wrote him—physically—into every novel. But I added my personality, because he was a bit of the pretty dumb blond of our family. I was scar face.

"Hey, stale coffee and old pizza is still preferable to Desdemona's breath, don't you think?" He stepped over old pizza boxes in an attempt to navigate down the hall to his bedroom. "Hold up, that ticket was front row, man. You promised to come. It's the last show tonight! What chick in the elevator?"

I plopped down in my computer chair and swung around like a little kid. Why was I still thinking about how that girl in the elevator smelled? I usually avoided women like the plague. Or maybe it was vice-versa. Dane had all the fun, and that was fine with me. We shared a common goal. The end would justify the means. Or that was what I kept telling myself. "Maybe I'll sneak in and grab a back row seat," I yelled down the hall, hoping to appease him. Better not to say that I had never intended on going to the show. Collecting the old newspapers, I began to systematically stack our scattered garbage. "She knew who we named Des after. I couldn't very well not give her the ticket. So say "hi" to her after the show. She thinks you're me. Don't impress her with your acting chops so much that she wants to jump you after the show, though. Capisce?"

As soon as the words were out of my mouth, I felt a pang in my chest. *Dane couldn't have her.* Whoa! I'd never had that thought before about a girl. I never cared who he chose to love and leave. After peeling off my winter hat designed to cover my cheek, I took a quick glance in the mirror by the front door and remembered why. I was ugly, and Dane was a Greek god. I brushed at the long scar running down the side of my cheek. No girl would ever want to be seen in public with me. That much was true.

"Why? Does she think this is a date?"

"No," I yelled my definitive answer so it reached his bedroom. Besides, no way I'd be able to make this den of men presentable enough to let a girl like Manda in here. Ever.

Who am I kidding? There was no room in my world for dating. Not now when I was so close. And Dane was a serial two-dater. Even if he liked her, he'd find some fatal flaw after the second date. Like Wendy with the overhanging second toe.

Damnit! I was drinking and had a copy of *Penthouse* in my grocery bag. Great first impression. So despite the fact I'd watched her for months, I'd kept quiet. And she never looked at me twice. My gut was beginning to tell me giving her that ticket was going to be a big mistake. And telling Dane this was *not* a date probably made him think that it was *for sure* a date.

Emerging from his bedroom in jeans and a gray Shakespeare T-shirt that read "These wenches cannot commit," he gave me a funny look. "What's up with you?"

"Nothing. Why don't we run lines for a bit?" My brother was magic on stage, and I was so proud of him. My lifelong fascination with Shakespeare made role-playing in our tiny apartment a hoot. I wished I could have his free conscience and reckless abandon on stage, but my nasty scar and PTSD kind of kept me typing instead of performing.

I'd died and sold my soul. My debt would never be repaid. My dirty life allowed me to let no one in. Maybe it was for the best. Dane was "the face" of our partnership, and I was the brains and the money.

After an hour, he asked me again, "You like this elevator girl or something? You're still acting weird." His gaze darted from my eyes to my scar and back. "You know not everyone judges a book by its cover. That scar isn't anything."

"So I'm not hideous. Geez, thanks." The scar was the visible sign of my outer ugliness. It was who I hated on the inside that was truly repulsive. I wanted to see that girl again. Maybe if she didn't know I was there… "It'll probably end up being an empty seat. And no, I don't *like* her."

A wicked twinkle appeared in my twin's eye. I knew what he was thinking. If I didn't like her, she wasn't off-limits to him. At that moment, I decided to go to the show—in case she actually went and fell for Dane's fake charm. My sewer life occasionally needed to be reminded of the flickers of beauty that could exist. Because each day I forgot about beauty more and more. I was drowning in a life I'd created and was out of control.

"Hey, after we run lines, do you want to order gyros from

Snickers, pick up some babes, bring them back here for some pre-show loving—?"

I held up my hand. "I pay girls plenty to entertain you when I need a demo, and how they navigate this cesspool of an apartment for a roll on your dirty sheets, I don't know. So no thanks. How about we clean up a little?"

"Lie to me again about how you don't like this elevator girl! What, are you scared I'm going to bring her up here? You've never cared about the state of our living quarters before." Dane began to pace, like he was a kindergartener putting together the pieces of a puzzle. He ticked things off on his fingers. "First, you pretend to be me. Then, you give a ticket to *my show* to a random woman in the elevator. Now, you want to clean?" Realization hit him. "You *do* like her!"

"She smells good." As soon as the words were out of my mouth, I regretted them and bolted for the safety of my bedroom. Desdemona lay sprawled out on my bed, and piles of books covered all my shelves and dressers.

Dane followed me, leaning his frame against my door. "Well, well, well. Mr. High-and-Mighty Smut Writer may actually be having some dirty thoughts of his own finally. Me likey!"

"Forget I said that. Look, I do need a demo of something called the "Cincinnati Bowtie" for my next scene. You up for that later tonight if I find some willing and ables?"

"Don't change the subject. Which girl? I'll bet it's the pink spandex-wearing jogger from the tenth floor."

I rolled my eyes and sat on the bed with Des, who grunted and rolled onto her back for some belly scratching. "Drop it. I'm serious. Just be polite if she comes tonight. For me."

"Because you're afraid she'll like me better?" Dane sniffed one of his armpits. "I might smell better than you, too. You sleep with a dog…literally."

"She won't like you once you aren't spouting Shakespeare, Bro."

"Touchy. Want to pull the old switcheroo? You take her to dinner then I'll sleep with her and see if she's goody-two-shoes enough for you? Your snake is so out of practice you probably don't even know how to use it anymore." The smirk on Dane's face made me want to wipe the smile right off of it.

"She's not like that."

"Wait, now you're defending someone you don't know? Sorry, but all women are like that, Bro! I'll bet you a crispy one-hundred dollar bill she begs me to bang her before the end of the night."

"You can't bring her here! She's a literary agent."

Dane rubbed his hands together. "Ah, the plot thickens. A literary agent who turns her nose up at erotica. I see." He picked up my latest tome that paid our rent and then some. "I hear you. I'll say we have bedbugs or something when she begs me to bed her after my stunning stage performance."

I opened a drawer and shoved a stack of bills in Dane's hand before I pushed past him to hit the shower. "Say 'hi' *if* she shows up. Go out wherever you want afterward, and try to stay out of trouble."

"Who, me?" Dane raised his eyebrows and placed a tepid hand over his heart.

I had to laugh. I couldn't help but love my brother.

But for some reason I couldn't explain, I wouldn't let her fall for Dane. I needed to get ready, because Dane was one of those people who only wanted what he couldn't have. And he couldn't get close to Manda. I didn't think I could handle it.

CHAPTER THREE

MANDA

"Thy friendship makes us fresh."
(King Henry the Sixth Part I 3.3.86)

After lunch with my dad, I cleaned like a frantic lunatic. In case… *In case, what?*

It wasn't like I'd invite the drunk Shakespeare sex addict guy up for a drink!

The place needed to be tidied up anyway. What would it hurt? After rearranging the hot pink fuzzy pillows on the sofa and re-stacking the timeless hardcover books on the coffee table, I placed a bottle of chardonnay in the fridge next to Maggie's champagne. *I can drink it alone,* I told myself. After the show. Because who was I to turn down a free ticket to see Shakespeare?

After a steamy, hot shower, I wrapped myself in a towel and called Maggie Monroe for the billionth time, only to leave yet another voice mail. Why would my number one author neglect my frantic calls? Where was that woman? The news repeatedly peppered throughout my frantic emails and excited voice mails should send her into fits of squealing and jumping for joy. After all our time and hard work…the *New York Times* Best Sellers list!

Leaving my phone within reach on my dresser, I dug through my drawers. As I suspected, nothing chic to wear to the theater.

Sifting through bras and undies, I picked out a cute matching set with little red hearts. Although my regular clothes might have said book nerd, I had a neurotic side that made me obsess over matching skivvies. At least no man would describe me as matronly—if a man ever got to see underneath my beloved collection of turtleneck sweater dresses. Not that I was about to let the sixth-floor hottie turned sixth-floor pin-up-loving-day-drunk into my boudoir.

Then why did my thoughts keep drifting back to him? What part could he have in a Shakespeare production anyway? Did he do the lighting or have a bit part? Either way, I couldn't deny his interest in Will Shakespeare and impromptu quoting of The Bard was a major turn-on.

Stop it! I chastised myself.

Pushing up my glasses, I clipped my still wet, messy blonde locks into my signature low, loose knot, pulled on one of my many black turtleneck sweater dresses, and slid into comfy flats. *This will do just fine. No need to primp for my now shattered version of the sixth-floor hottie.*

The reflection in the floor-length mirror frowned back at me. I stood on my tiptoes. Heels would be sexier and elongate my legs and all that, but I'd trip and kill myself for sure. Plus, who knew how far I'd need to walk? Limping in pain or having a twisted ankle from a sewer grate wasn't worth it, was it?

Ugh! Why was I trying to impress this guy?

Even after adding a skinny belt for a touch of flair, the whole ensemble—my go-to for client dinners, book signings, and conferences—fell flat. "I look perfect for the theater and then a trip to…the library," I told Beefer. Several attempts of claustrophobia-inducing scarves and painful dangling earrings later, I gave up the fight.

"Oh well, Beefer, I don't wear sexy lingerie from La Perla. Or fancy designer dresses. If I never find a guy who likes me for the sweatpants-loving, glasses-wearing nerd I am, he's simply not for me. Besides," I said, patting his fuzzy head, "a prerequisite is loving you…La Furla."

Beefer rolled over, and his vehement panting rocked the entire bed. "Who's got hundreds of dollars for bras, underwear, dresses, and shoes? Not me. I'm more of a clearance rack girl, you know?" I spoke to Beefer, believing he understood everything I said.

I snuck another peek in the mirror at the sensible outfit. Why was it easier to decorate an apartment than a human body? My buzzer rang. "Hi, George." I spoke into the call box.

"A Miss Vanessa is here to see you."

"Thanks. Send her up!"

Five minutes later, Vanessa flung open the door to my apartment, and Beefer ran to meet her. "Sweet Jesus, Manda, can't you text me back, like, ever?" Vanessa huffed.

My desire to hear an actual voice rather than read sloppy shorthand prompted me to wait for Vanessa to contact me the old-fashioned way…with a visit or a phone call. She hated it. My bestie lived and worked in the city. Engaged to a mature investment banker and set to be married in an extraordinarily expensive wedding next spring, she had the material world at her fingertips. But I loved her anyway.

Vanessa was one of those people for whom nothing was ever enough. She was five foot eight, model thin with shiny stick-straight black hair with plum highlights. She didn't own sweatpants, which I could attest to because we were matched as roommates in the freshmen dorms. After rooming together for four years, we graduated as love-ya-like-a-sister forever friends even though we were as different as a race car and a minivan. We both turned twenty-seven this year, single and childless. The only girl from college I still talked to that was married with children was our other friend, Ally.

"I am in desperate need of outfit assistance. I'm going to the theater and need to look—"

"You can't wear that." Vanessa interrupted.

My cheeks got warm. "Why not?"

"Wait, is this a date?"

"Not really. This guy on the elevator—"

"Elevator?" Vanessa's laugh was like a contagious sneeze.

"I know it's crazy." I closed my eyes, imagining him spouting off more Shakespearean quotes.

"Well, I'll need to assess the assets of Elevator Man, so bring him to Rocket afterward." She paused. "Babycakes, I love you, but put your contacts in and let that gorgeous hair down!"

"I consider my sophisticated low bun and my glasses flattering. And no, it's not a date!"

Giving me a gentle shove into the bathroom, she pressed, "Put some damn contacts in, and get your ass out here so I can do your hair."

"Okay. But I want him to like *me*, not some fake me." I complied and popped in my contacts. Vanessa's assistance would be invaluable, no doubt about that. "You're the one with the body of Jessica Alba." I shook my head. Good thing I loved Vanessa and knew her outward appearance was a cover for the kind, generous person she was inside. And when her loaded fiancé was away, Vanessa loved to grab Ally and the three of us would go out and regale each other with college party stories.

I stuck my head out of the bathroom with one contact in and one to go. "Did I tell you one of my authors hit the *New York Times* Best Sellers list?" My phone *still* had nothing from Maggie. I'd have to fly out and knock on her door if she ignored me much longer. Where in the world was that woman? We had big stuff to plan! Big. Stuff.

"That is amazing!" She slid open the door to my closet. "Hey, what have you been saving this for?" The flimsy ebony-colored silk dress still had the tags on because I was debating taking it back.

She hung the dress over my door and placed the one insanely high pair of heels I owned beneath the dress to complete the outfit.

"No way. I can't pull that off."

"Just try it on! You could even wear it with my Giuseppe Zanotti open toe slash booties." She slipped off her own shoes and put on a pair of my fuzzy slippers.

"I don't even know the language you're speaking right now," I huffed, tugging off my uber comfy sweater dress. "But I'll appease you so you can say I'm right." This was like getting ready to go out in college all over again.

"At least you've listened to me in the lingerie department, and whatever workout you're doing has given you a slammin' body, sister." Vanessa circled me like I was a piece of meat on display.

"Thanks?" I blushed even though I was pretty proud of my new kettlebell workout and intermittent fasting mantra. "You're the one who yammered on about workplace panty lines being a crime."

"When a man finally appreciates your hot librarian look, he'll be pleasantly surprised."

No more stalling. The impromptu runway show began.

Backless. Braless. My heels. Her booties. Jangling jewelry. On and on to perfect the look.

I wobbled around my bedroom while we giggled, and Vanessa finally conceded that the trusty old sweater dress was the way to go...if I wore her boots.

"Can't say we didn't give it the old college try! At least let me do your hair and makeup." She turned her head toward me and waggled her eyebrows. "Pleeease?"

I hopped up off the bed and lunged for the sweater dress. "No time, sunshine! It's nary an hour until showtime. Any guy will have to appreciate schlumpy me to get through to sexy me." I held my arms out and gave my upper half a shake.

"Oh boy," Vanessa laughed. "That's sexy you?"

"Yup, it's in here somewhere." I looked under my arms and over my shoulders. "I'm sure of it. Not everyone has their cleaning lady put their vibrator in the dishwasher," I reminded her. No way I'd ever let her live down the day she sent me for wine glasses and I found her...thing right there in the dishwasher next to her good wine glasses!

"You're right, not everyone is as lucky as I am Now, sit. At least let me brighten up those beautiful eyes and work on that hair." She pulled out hair contraptions and clips before spraying my hair with dry shampoo and heat protector. Then she applied eyelid primer before tackling my unruly locks and minimalist makeup job. I sat still like a good girl and let her work the usual magic.

While she pushed and pulled on hair follicles and eyelashes, I told her the latest on my dear old brother, Pete.

"So the poor guy is shopping for lingerie for *his wife* at work? So what? Close your eyes." Soft brushes tickled my eyelids. "Now open and look up."

I watched the ceiling fan above the bed, trying to catch one of the blades in the rotation and force it into focus. I didn't dare say a word until she was done lest she blind me with a mascara wand. "It probably wouldn't be such a big deal if he wasn't the pastor of his church and the church secretary hadn't caught him. Apparently, the whole congregation is up in arms."

"And Sarah?"

I didn't know what Pete's wife had said. But I was taking a guess that she wasn't being overly supportive. "No idea."

Vanessa could not conceal her sly smile. "So the old Petey is finally back? Aw, hell, he's just a typical guy. And shopping for lingerie isn't exactly watching porn. What he did was innocent enough. Besides, all men that have the internet—so all men—have seen something naughty online. Look, unless it's a three-hour a day ignore-your-wife, quit-your-day-job habit, who cares? Don't women read sexy romance books or fantasize about real people, like their coworkers? Is that any better?" Vanessa asked.

The coffee pot scuttle at my office was always about the married guy at the front desk who apparently appeared in many a coworker's recurring fantasies. "I guess not. But the church secretary most likely does not share your viewpoint."

The eyelash curler appeared. "Do you have to do that?"

"Yes and don't squirm."

The torturous device was crimped on my poor, unsuspecting eyelashes.

"That's better. One more coat of mascara."

Willing my eyes not to water, I let her continue.

"Can I call him Porno Pete next time I see him?" Vanessa teased.

Oh, great. I shouldn't have told her. "Please don't, and put down that color lipstick or we are going to have a chick fight. I'm serious!"

Hands up, Vanessa backed away and rummaged through endless lipstick tubes until she selected a nude color with a hint of pink.

I gave a quick nod. Acceptable.

"Want more of my thoughts on men?"

Afraid to protest lest I become the Joker, I nodded.

"Open your mouth a little." She took a deep breath. "I fight with Geoffrey about money and sex. I mean, I love sex.

I'm open to having some consensual fun in the boudoir. Too bad he's such a bore. He'd never shop for lingerie online with me, even if I begged."

"And that's a bad thing?" That was low on my list of to-dos with any boyfriend. Ever.

"No. It's not the worst thing, but it's another thing on a growing list. He refuses to volunteer with me at the food pantry, says he doesn't want to catch a weird disease from a bum." She paused. "I think I might break off the engagement." Vanessa whispered the words as though the thought had just occurred to her.

"Oh my gosh." I jumped up and gave her a tight hug. "Are you sure?"

Vanessa cleared her throat while she put my makeup away. "Don't worry about me. I'll figure it out. I'm sure it's pre-wedding jitters. Anyway, how about a little advice while embarking on your *first* date in a while? Don't be so fast to judge. Wait until the third date," she teased.

I made a face. "Very funny. It's not a date. You want to talk about you and Geoffrey?"

"Not remotely. Now, don't trip, but try to back up and do a spin."

That I could handle.

"You look amazing." Glancing down at my slippers on her feet, she added, "You think my doorman will recognize me?"

I took one careful step after another, adjusting to the height of the boots. "Answer me this: Is Geoffrey the man of your dreams?" I grabbed my purse and wobbled the whole way to the door.

Vanessa's eyes got glassy. "You're killing me today with questions! I honestly don't know. I do know with enough sex and booze, I'm pretty happy most of the time."

I put on my coat and gave her a peck on the cheek. "You know you're my best friend, but that's a terrible answer. Maybe you should deal with this Geoffrey thing sooner rather than later." I tapped my ring finger to remind her of the honking rock she was wearing.

"Yeah, yeah, I'm on it. Now scram, you. Have fun with the sixth-floor hottie, and give him a real shimmie. I'll be at Rocket later. If you want, bring him there."

Beefer padded to the door, and Vanessa scratched him on the head. "I'll let him out and lock up. You better move it or you're going to be late."

"Thanks, Vanessa. For everything." Opening the door of the apartment, I gave her one last look. We had to hash this out soon. Before she sashayed down the aisle. The return look she gave me was sad. This girl was not the party animal socialite she let others think she was.

"Knock him dead with your sensible clothes and knowledge of the Bard," Vanessa yelled after me with a wave before she shut the door.

Outside my building, the smell of stale cigarettes and frothy beer wafted from the corner bar, Snickers, a place I avoided like the plague. Every night the bar held a plethora of too-young, too-drunk boys whose hormones leapt to attention whenever fresh blood entered their territory, whether that was a pretty girl to harass or a non-local boy to provoke into a skirmish.

I'd sooner exchange chain letters with a guy in jail than pick up a guy in there.

Peeking inside, I half expected to see the sixth-floor hottie —*wait, should I still call him that?*—sitting on a barstool with his name on it.

I hailed a cab and jumped in. The show started in thirty minutes. "Navy Pier, please. And quickly," I told the driver. My phone rang, so I rustled around in my bag to answer it. "Hello?"

"Miss Wolfgram?" The man's voice sobered me immediately.

"Speaking."

"Are you Maggie Monroe's agent?"

"I am. Who's this?" My star author better not have broken her other leg before we could go out and celebrate.

"This is Ms. Monroe's lawyer. I'm sorry to be the one to tell you, but Ms. Monroe passed away yesterday afternoon."

I was speechless. Had I heard him wrong?

"Miss Wolfgram, are you still there?"

"Yes." The words caught in my throat.

"As you know, Ms. Monroe was recovering from a broken leg. A blood clot from her leg got to her lungs. I'm sorry to have to call you with this information, but as her lawyer, we need to be in touch regarding subsequent book royalties from the publisher, which will need to be forwarded to the next of kin."

My heart sank. "Of course, thank you."

"I'm sorry to have bothered you on a weekend, but her husband said you'd want to know. I'll be preparing the necessary paperwork and will call you again next week."

"All right. Thank you, goodbye." With nothing left to say, I slipped the phone back in my purse. Maggie never read the emails. She died never knowing she'd finally made it big—hit the *New York Times* Best Sellers list and was on the verge of the success she'd always dreamed of. But that didn't matter anymore. With Maggie gone, the *Pink Cupcake Princess* series was also dead. Poor Maggie would never enjoy her hard-won success. And there would be no sequels.

Poor Maggie. How could this be? Maggie wasn't just my client. I considered her my friend.

The taxi screeched to a stop, and my body rocked forward. A glowing sign read Chicago Shakespeare Theater. Handing over the first twenty-dollar bill I could find, I didn't wait for change and stepped onto Navy Pier with a shiver, my mind a fog of confusion and fear. Harsh wind burned my cheeks as the sun's winter warmth turned to a brisk lakeshore chill.

Brisk Lake Michigan air filled my lungs. Fishermen lined the pier, some fishing for pleasure and others for necessity. Seagulls squawked overhead, flying low and hovering in the air, hoping to catch scraps or discarded bait before the sun set. It was a late winter with only a dusting of snow at the end of November. But real winter…was coming.

I should have gone home, but something dragged me into the theater. Probably denial that any of this was real. Crowds of theatergoers ferried me through the main door into familiar albeit surreal surroundings. Voices echoed around me, individual words imperceptible. People appeared insubstantial, like ethereal ghosts. One day, every person in this crowd would be dead—like Maggie.

Like my mother.

And for what?

The mob oozed toward the theater entrance. An usher took my ticket and led me to a front row seat on the aisle.

Maggie couldn't be dead.

A piece of me said to get up, go home, and sob into Beefer's fur. But another piece of me wanted to forget everything and let the theater act as a temporary escape from this new reality. A deep breath helped to pull me back to the present moment.

What could I do for Maggie right now? Nothing. Settling into my seat, I tried so hard to push down this fresh pain like I'd done every time I entered Mom's bedroom after school all those years ago. Knowing every day time was against us. I donned a brave facade solely for Mom's sake, even though she saw right through me. "I'll be fine, Mom. Yes, I'll take care of Dad." Like the movie *Groundhog Day*, except one day after school, Mom's bed was empty.

Thoughts of Maggie and Mom got tangled up, vying for

time in my dizzy head.

I had lost track of time when the house lights dimmed and the announcer said, "Please turn off your phones, and enjoy tonight's performance of *Romeo and Juliet*." A tragedy. Great, more tragedy. And here I was trapped in the front row.

With no idea what part the sixth-floor hottie drunk played in bringing this production to fruition, it caught me completely off guard when Romeo entered stage left.

Uh-oh. The sixth-floor hottie was *Romeo*!

Mesmerized, I sank into the cushy seat and let the play seep into my bones. For the moment, my grief about Maggie shoved away. My nerves were raw, so I let the play do what it was supposed to do…carry me away.

It wasn't just his change of clothes or boyish hairdo; it wasn't simply the words he recited or the expert stage direction. When an actor was good, the audience let themselves fall in love with the character. Three stair steps separated the stage and my feet. In one scene, Romeo took the first and then the second step off the stage and sank down directly in front of me. He leaned on his elbows.

I forgot to blink and held my breath when he began a short soliloquy, absorbing his every inflection, intonation, gesture, and emotion. When he kissed Juliet, I thought, *It should be me he's kissing*. In the safe, darkened venue, I became Juliet and lived alongside him in a perfect two-hour fantasy.

A deep well of sadness started low in the pit of my stomach and worked its way up, bubbling from a place deep inside me —a place where rationality lost to raw emotion, sanity lost to blind devotion, and practicality lost to sheer madness. I could do nothing to push the emotions back down.

I missed my mom.

Maggie was dead.

And the look Romeo gave Juliet… Maybe just once, I needed a man to look at me like that…for real.

CHAPTER FOUR

HARRY

"All the world 's a stage,
and all the men and women merely players:
They have their exits and their entrances;
And one man in his time plays many parts,"
(As You Like It 2.7.140-42)

Even from my seat in the back, I saw her. Manda. She looked...off. Shaky. Not paying attention. A deep well of sadness emanated from the woman I'd met in the elevator a few hours ago, who now sat half a theater away. The tension in my body unfurled.

My brother commanded the stage, but I couldn't take my eyes off of Manda.

What was she thinking?

Did she recognize Dane as me?

Maybe she thought I looked silly in padded slippers and green tights that led to baggy bloomers and a loose, cream-colored tunic. The front ties of Dane's tunic hung open, revealing his shaved chest. I watched her straighten in her seat.

She'd recognized Dane, with his thick hair slicked down by copious amounts of gel to detract from his real age to play this character. His spoken lines reverberated through the theater. To me, it was like listening to the sound of my own voice tape-recorded and played back. One critic had written that Dane Sackes "played Romeo with a joking edge to the character's morose obsession with love and death." We had high-fived over the glowing review.

Every flinch, every shift in her seat, I watched. My level of concentration was zero for the play itself and focused solely on this woman.

I settled in, thinking about how it had come to this. My sister. The deal with the devil. The life that was no longer my own. The two steps forward and five steps back of the mission. There was no denying this leading a double life shit was for the birds. I wanted to be free. But I'd never be free. The past would never be undone. My path had been set in motion long ago, and I had no choice in the matter anymore.

I'd never once been distracted by anything. Or anyone.

Until now.

In the elevator, she'd smelled so good.

But deep down, I knew it could never be.

How could life be utterly changed in one instant? For one wrong or right decision, life played out like it was a stage. Romance. Tragedy. No changing of history.

She would shake his hand after the performance, and all three of us would go our separate ways. But I knew I would never stop obsessing. Never stop watching. Never stop hoping.

When Dane died on stage, he did a good job of it. I had to admit it.

When the house lights went up, I stayed right where I was. Then I saw it. My dear old brother making his way toward her.

That was the moment my whole life changed.

CHAPTER FIVE

MANDA

"O Romeo, Romeo! Wherefore art thou Romeo?"
(Romeo and Juliet 2.1.75)

The image of Romeo slumped on the stage floor seared itself into my brain.

The play was over and the audience had leapt to its feet, roaring and clapping with thunderous ovation. That's when I began to cry. Not the tears-running-down-your-face, wipe-them-away-so-no-one-notices crying, but the embarrassing I-wish-I-wasn't-in-public crying. More like the loud hiccups-of-air, unstoppable type of crying. My vision blurred, nose ran, chest heaved, and my breaths came in short, labored pants.

The chattering crowd filtered out of the theater while I remained with my head swirling with visions of my mother's funeral, Maggie having a cocktail at lunch, and Romeo falling to the ground in front of me. I wept for perfect love, life lost, broken hearts, perfect books, Shakespearian prose, and...

"I know I'm a great actor, but really..."

I couldn't bring myself to lift my head.

"What's the matter?"

A hand squeezed my shoulder.

Without a thought, I stood up and threw my arms around him. "Maggie Monroe's dead."

He held me with the strength a woman yearned for when she was weak. I pressed my whole body against his, lost in his warm, protective embrace.

"I know it feels like we've known each other forever, but remind me again, who's Maggie Monroe?"

I pushed back from him, collecting myself. This was like dealing with an entirely different person from the guy on the elevator. "I'm sorry. I got a call right before the show. My friend died, and then watching you die onstage—"

His forehead wrinkled in concern, and he rubbed my cheek and looked at me like Juliet was nothing more than a damp washcloth compared to me. The look only lasted for a split second. "Let's duck out the back door and go for a drink. You can tell me all about it." He snagged my hand and tugged us away from the main exit.

"Shouldn't you go to the lobby? Your fans—"

"No worries." Backstage, he grabbed a duffel bag, and we hailed a cab with him still sporting his full Romeo regalia.

"I'm in a cab with Romeo," I said, checking my mascara-streaked face in a compact. "I never want to watch you die onstage again."

His smile was a tad cocky as he winked at me. "I'll promise you no such thing. I'm a Shakespearian actor. Sword scenes and dying on stage is my gig. But let's make a pit stop at our building so I can change."

When the cab stopped, he looked at me. "Want to split this?"

I shook my head and paid the cabbie. He jumped out and never turned around to give me a hand. But I didn't mind.

We pushed through the revolving doors one right after the

other into the lobby of the condo. A man heaved a deep sigh then slumped over, holding his head in his hands on one of the sofas in our lobby.

I stopped cold. It was my brother, Pete, surrounded by mounds of suitcases. "Uh-oh. That's my brother."

Romeo—whose real name I now realized I didn't know—gave me a flourished bow. "I'll go change my clothes and let you two talk. When I come back down, you can decide if you still want to have that drink." With a wink, Romeo turned and headed for the elevators.

Moving as quickly as I could without breaking an ankle, I hurried over to Pete. "What happened?" I asked.

My brother looked like hell. His unshaven face, ratty T-shirt, and dirty jeans gave him a slept-in-his-car look. His dirty blond hair was disheveled, and the normally arched eyebrow that preceded his snide remarks drooped with the rest of his body. Even though he was only three years my senior, he looked like a well-worn forty rather than his normal, meticulously groomed thirty.

"Sarah kicked me out." His face was still buried in his hands. "I just called Dad. He's on his way down."

CHAPTER SIX

HARRY

"I'll budge not an inch"
(The Taming of the Shrew 1.1.13)

Back inside the condo, I paced. Furious. What the hell was Dane thinking?

Then, the key turned and Dane came skipping in like a kid with a new toy.

"Hey," I marched up to him. "What happened? You hugged her and left with her?"

"Easy, tiger." He went to his room to change, and I followed him, shoving open the door he'd partially closed behind him. "I'm only taking her out for some drinks. Someone died, and I *moved* her on stage. She's with her brother in the lobby. The poor thing needs some comforting, Sackes style if you know what I mean." He made a thrusting motion with his hips.

For the first time in my life, I wanted to punch my brother in the face. "Dane, it was me who met her in the elevator. I gave her the ticket. If anyone is taking her out for a drink, it's me!" The volume in my voice was too high.

Obviously startled, my brother paused. "But—"

"Mine." I felt the growl in my throat. "I will take her out. You will go find an easy girl at the bar. Someone more your style."

Throwing his clothes on the ground, Dane moved toward me and gave me a push. "You're being an asshole. What difference does it make who beds Miss Goodie Two-shoes? She's not your type at all."

"But she's *your* type?" My words came out with a bite I had long kept in check. Years of regrets. Years of built-up resentment. After all the women I'd paid to bring up to our place. With all the dirty deals I'd made to get us closer and closer to the prize. "Who says I have a type? When was the last time I ever asked you for anything? It's me who makes all the sacrifices. You live in the limelight and have everything. I'm only asking you for one thing. This one girl is not for you."

Dane held out his hand. "How much? How much is it worth to you to keep me away from her? She loves Shakespeare. I'm the Shakespearean actor. Not you."

I shook my head. "You want money to stay away from her? You disgust me. If it wasn't for me—"

"If it wasn't for you, Harry, *both* our lives would be very different."

His words stopped me in my tracks. Because he was speaking the truth. I backed up, went into my room, and grabbed my lockbox. Opening it, I threw it in his room. Bills spilled onto his floor, and change clattered on his desk and dresser. "Take it all. Take her. Take everything. You're right. I'm the piece of shit that deserves nothing. I'm to blame for all of it."

Stomping into the kitchen, I opened a bottle of whiskey

and took a long drink. The burning felt good. Felt evil, like the liquid belonged inside me.

I stared at the one picture on our refrigerator of the three of us. Then there was an arm on my shoulder. I brushed him away and took another drink before heading out to the balcony. I gulped in the cold air, letting the shakes come. Allowing my well-deserved pain to take control of me once again.

"Hey," Dane spoke softly. "I'm sorry. That was out of line. I'll tell you everything that happened. Go take her somewhere quiet and console her. You are right about one thing."

Shooting him a look, I had to ask, "What's that?"

"She does smell good."

CHAPTER SEVEN

MANDA

*"Our doubts are traitors
And make us lose the good we oft might win
By fearing to attempt."
(Measure for Measure 1.4.77-78)*

Dad did not look happy when he got to the lobby. He gave us both a hard look.

"Sarah kicked him out." I tried to keep my voice low.

"Why?" Dad drew out the word, now sporting a wrinkled brow.

Pete moaned and covered his face. "I don't want to talk about it."

"Well, you're sure as hell going to talk about it." When Dad spoke in that tone, we generally knew better than to kid around.

Pete fumbled with the tags on one of his massive suitcases. "Something happened at work, and I might lose my job." His voice was barely a whisper. "Can we talk somewhere else?"

The lobby was barren. Even George, ever in vigil at the

main desk, must have been on a break. "No. Tell me now," Dad said.

Pete hung his head like a puppy who'd peed on the rug. "It was no big deal, really. I think my secretary just—she…she kind of walked in on me using my computer to look at…stuff I shouldn't have been looking at."

I had a bad habit of trying to lighten situations with alliteration. "Preacher Pete not preaching peace but pilfering through…porn?"

"Shut up, Manda. I was shopping for lingerie for Sarah, not looking at dirty websites."

"Good God, Peter. At work? What were you thinking?" Dad rolled his head, and his neck cracked before he heaved a fatherly sigh. "Is this a bigger problem? Something you need to"—he cleared his throat—"get help with?"

Pete shrugged his shoulders. "No. I just royally screwed up. But—"

"But nothing, Son," he interrupted. "You can bring your bags upstairs and stay with me on the sole condition you call Sarah and find a way to make this right. Otherwise, take those bags and go back out the same revolving doors you just came in."

When Colonel Wolfgram came out, there was no arguing with the man. He was as practical as he was pragmatic.

Pete stared at the front door as if considering making a break for it. "It's really not that big of a—"

"When was the last time you ate, Son?" Dad laid a gentle hand on his shoulder.

"Yesterday."

I piped up. "I'll run out and get sandwiches." This sounded like a topic the men should discuss first before I threw in my two cents, which would really amount to a ha'penny seeing as my opinion on the matter wouldn't be considered by Pete's wife or his congregation.

"What about your date?" Pete asked.

"You've got a date?"

Great, now Dad's attention was on me. I shot Pete a mind-your-own-business look. "It's not a date."

"You go have fun, kiddo. I need Petey alone for a bit." Not waiting for my response, Dad headed for the elevator, already pulling two of Pete's suitcases behind him.

"See you later, Sis." Pete gave me a brotherly smack on the back. "A date, huh? Where does he go to church?"

Crossing my arms, I gave him my best glare. "I'm not going. And really? Like you're in a position to ask. Very funny. Almost as funny as the headlines of your small-town newspaper that are about to read: 'Preacher Peeks at Porn Prior to Pontificating on Properly Praising the Pious.'"

"Why do you taunt me?"

"Because I love you, this will all work out, and that's what sisters do. Now scram. And good luck with Dad." With enough on their plates, I didn't feel like it was the time to go into details about Maggie's death.

I pushed the "up" button on the elevator. "Sorry, but I'm ditching Romeo. You need me. I can't let you leave me with your slouched shoulders saddled with spiritual sadness."

"Manda, I'm warning you," Pete said with the hint of a twinkle in his eye.

My every-parents-dream older brother had nixed me from dating all kinds of people in high school, approving only rogue members of the chess team and theater geeks who fostered my love of men who could hold intelligent conversations and regale me with stories from the last thing they'd read. *In a book.*

Considering the school jocks rarely read anything except CliffsNotes and the sports pages, he'd done me an immense favor and an utter disservice. I was now pickier with guys than Jerry Seinfeld with his revulsion for soup-scented women. Ever since high school, I scoured the planet for the impossible…a highly intelligent and compassionate man, who'd be fiercely loyal with the brawn to back it up and knee-shaking, breath-hitching, I-need-to-change-my-panties attractiveness to boot. For the record, no man had ever made me do that, but I held out hope.

That was who my imagination weaved into the sixth-floor hottie.

Now, a veritable figment of my imagination.

Oh, lest a strong handshake be forgotten. I never trusted a weak handshake. Better to grow old and die educated than drop my standards for a fake, self-serving jackass.

The door to the stairwell opened at the same time as the elevator. Pete blocked me from getting in. "Wait for your date. Go have fun. I'll be fine." Pete winked, and the elevator door shut without me on the inside.

"We have to stop meeting by the elevator." Romeo, now in street wear with Wolverine-esque sideburns saw George return from his break with a swish of the front door. He grabbed my hand and led me to the front desk.

George furrowed his eyebrows at us.

The long strips reminded me of the fuzzy caterpillars we caught as kids. "Good evening, George. Would you be so kind as to hail us a cab?"

I pulled my hand out of his. "I'm sorry. I can't go. There's a family drama happening upstairs, and they need me." I paused but couldn't help myself from adding, "You have sideburns?"

"Velcro. You like?" He tugged at one of them to show me they were fake. "I can't have the paparazzi chasing me after the show, you know."

The front desk phone rang, and George held up one finger to us. "Hello? Yes, they are. Of course. I'll tell her. Yes, sir. He is a quality fellow. I can vouch for him." He winked at Romeo and hung up the phone. "Miss Wolfgram, your father said you are not needed upstairs right now and ordered you to go on your date."

"See?" Wolverine Romeo said. "And George even put in a good word to your old man for me. I will not abandon a woman who a short while ago was sobbing in my arms. Sounds like your family drama can wait. I should know. Are you ready for a little wining, dining, and—?"

I got a whiff of whiskey on his breath. Why would George vouch for this guy? "No. I'm going to bed. I'm sure you have magazines to keep you company." Elevator Romeo was back. *I'm out. Drop the mic.*

"Nonsense! One drink and I'll personally tuck you in bed." He grabbed my hand once again and led me through the revolving doors all the while with George not helping me escape.

"George, save me!" I cried, not able to hide my disbelief.

Our beloved doorman laughed and actually gave me a push forward! "He's a good guy, Manda. I promise. You kids go out and have some fun."

"If I'm found dead in a dumpster, you better explain this to my father!" I yelled back at a grinning George before I found myself whisked through the revolving doors and ushered into a waiting cab.

When the traitorous doorman stepped outside and I looked back, he tipped his hat. They were in cahoots! I was done for.

CHAPTER EIGHT

HARRY

"But I will wear my heart upon my sleeve
For daws to peck at. I am not what I am."
(Othello 1.1.64)

As soon as we were in close proximity inside the cab, I began to panic. Every fiber of my being wanted to understand her inner workings, which was totally unlike me. My usual devil-may-care attitude was getting a makeover. My mind raced. Should I suggest the Crimson Lounge or the rooftop bar at the Wit? I wanted to impress her—not *I have money* or *I'm sophisticated* impress her, but take her somewhere to talk. Like real people.

For the first time in a really long time, I was nervous. *Don't come on too strong. But don't be weak.* I drank in her scent, which was filling the cab. "We could get a drink at Crimson or the Wit or—"

"I told my friend Vanessa we might meet her out, but I'm not sure I'm up for that level of excitement—she usually hangs out at Rocket."

I shook my head. "That meat market? How about somewhere quiet?" *No way. No how.* The idea of her inside a place like that with the male-sharks circling her made my skin crawl and my fists clench. I'd have to beat the shit out of any man who looked the wrong way at her.

"To tell you the truth, I'm starving. Pizza?" she suggested.

Straightforward with brevity. I could appreciate that. "As you wish."

"Gino's East?"

I breathed a sigh of relief at her suggestion. She liked pizza. I liked pizza. Food compatibility test. Check. "Can you at least attempt to be a little high maintenance so I don't fall madly in love with you until our third date?" I teased. "C'mon, twist the knife. Do you like beer?"

"'I would give all my fame for a pot of ale,'" she quoted Henry the fifth and winked. "Seriously, I'd take a cold beer over a cosmo any day."

"You're killing me here, Manda."

She retrieved the *Romeo and Juliet* program from her purse. "Nice to make your acquaintance…Dane Sackes." She stuck out her hand. And wouldn't it be my luck, a handshake firm as cement. Another thing I liked in a woman.

We ducked inside Gino's East, one of the best pizza joints in Chitown. Graffiti covered the dark walls as did autographed pictures from celebrities who'd paid homage to the pizza here. The place was jam-packed, as always. "Table for two. Upstairs."

The dark-haired hostess looked overworked and unappreciated. "I can take your name. The wait time is about an hour and a half." She blinked, at the ready with a pen to jot down our names.

"Well, we're starving. I know you have some room. Somewhere." I slipped her a hundred-dollar bill and leaned in, whispering, "I'm a friend of Vito's." She disappeared for a moment and returned with Vito, who gave me a quick nod and led us upstairs.

"A little old for you, isn't she?" Vito muttered under his breath.

"Business." I hated to use my connections because owing anyone a favor was a bad idea, but tonight, I didn't care.

With shocked looks from the packed waiting room, Manda scampered up the steps behind me to a small vacant table that awaited us. Vito left us, and a hostess wiped off the table, lit a candle, and pulled out a chair for Manda. "Your server tonight is Josh, and don't hesitate to let me know if you need anything." The hostess knew better than to question Vito and left without another passing glance.

"Money talks, I guess." Manda's tone was half-annoyed and half-elated. "I'm happy we don't have to wait until the end of time to get a pizza, but how did you do that?"

"Money is paper and does what it's supposed to do. Currency and nothing more. Speaking of doing, do you want to talk about your friend, Maggie?"

She sat with her legs crossed, the top one bouncing a bit and hitting the underside of our table. She blinked repeatedly. Maybe I should have waited to bring this up, but I had an immediate and urgent need to know what was wrong and how I could fix it. Her gorgeous legs led up to the knitted black dress that looked like a cozy sweater. She left a lot up to my imagination.

Before she could answer, the waiter checked in. "Hi, I'm Josh. Can I get you two started tonight with something to drink?"

"I'll have a Corona with a lime," Manda said. "Please."

"Make it two," I added.

The waiter rushed off to collect our drinks. When he returned, she squeezed the lime, pushed it inside her bottle, and took a sip.

"How do you make swigging from a beer bottle look so damn sexy?"

Setting her beer down, her face turned the cutest shade of crimson. "I'm the furthest thing from sexy. And I'm sure you've seen many a girl drink from a beer bottle."

"I've seen them do a lot more than that." I leaned in closer. As soon as the words were out of my mouth, I knew it was too much. I was scaring her.

She cleared her throat with a deliberate subject change, clearly uncomfortable with my intensity. But I couldn't help it. She had…something. Something that twisted my guts in knots and made my chest tighten so I could barely breathe. This woman was like my favorite buzz. I felt drunk before I even threw back the first beer.

But how long could I hide the truth? It's not like I could really date her anyway. I refused to drag any woman into the cesspool of danger that was my life. And she'd never understand. But for tonight, I decided to forget about that.

The waiter reappeared and took our pizza order. I let her order whatever she wanted. Pizza and mushrooms. I hated mushrooms, but for her, I'd eat them.

The air between us was thick, and she cut it. "So, how long have you been acting?"

"Since I got the role of Puck in *A Midsummer Night's Dream* in high school," I lied. "When the acting bug bit, his fangs went deep and haven't let me go yet." Much better. I watched her relax.

"I hope they never do. You have a stage presence and way of bringing the words to life that made it hard for me to even blink. I didn't want to miss anything."

I slung an arm over the back of the chair. "Actors are insecure. Our oxygen is positive feedback. Honestly, I assume I suck on stage. What do I really do anyway? Someone tells me where to stand, what to wear, and what to say." I paused. "But for some reason, your praise is inflating me more than any kind words from my director, stage manager, reviewers, or fellow actors. You emanate authority. I like that."

I barely noticed when the pizza arrived. She told me about her family: Her mom died when she was in school, her dad lived in the building, and her brother, whom Dane had passed in the lobby, was a pastor who was in town due to some marital strife.

All was well enough until she tried to steer the conversation back to me. "So, do you have any brothers or sisters?"

"Have. Did. What book shaped your life the most?" Questions deftly dodged if I did say so myself. She took the hint and continued telling me about herself. I found out we both loved the Cubs and walking our dogs.

"So you really named your dog Desdemona?"

I laughed. "Of course I did. As you found out today, I'm quite the Shakespeare aficionado."

"So was Maggie." Reaching for her purse, she dug out her phone. "I'm really sorry to do this in the middle of dinner, but I have to let Mr. Peddet know what happened, even though I still don't believe it myself." She tapped out a text on her phone and put it back in her purse.

"Your boss is Roger Peddet? As in the Roger Peddet Literary Agency?"

"Yes, that's who I work for." She took a deep breath, ready to broach the subject. "Right before your show, I found out one of my authors—and a longtime friend—died suddenly. And she *just* made the *New York Times* Best Sellers list for one of her children's books. I don't know if she even got the news before..." Her voice trailed off.

"I'm so sorry." I grabbed her hand and gave it a squeeze. I couldn't resist. I wished I could take away her pain, never mind my own. A bolt of electricity passed between us. She must have felt it because she jerked her head up and stared right at me.

"She died before knowing she'd finally made it big."

"Life's not fair; that much I'll tell you." *Understatement.*

"Her husband lost his job in the recession, and they were relying solely on royalty checks to pay the bills. The two of them had even joked about a franchise with princess tea parties and cupcakes. Now he'll have to bury that idea alongside Maggie." A sad smile crossed her face. "She was the first author I ever signed."

How ironic that I was falling fast for a literary agent. Her words tickled the frayed fringes of my thoughts, and I pushed the idea down. It was a terrible idea. Bad for everyone. Even though I knew I could help her. "So that's the Maggie you were talking about?"

She nodded, finishing the last of her beverage.

I flagged down Josh, our waiter. "My date needs another beer."

"Absolutely," he said, neatly clearing away the plates and empty bottles. "How was your pizza?"

"The best, as always," I answered before noticing that Josh hadn't asked *us* how the pizza was. He'd asked Manda's tits. Or, at least, the hint of them under that tight black sweater.

He leaned over her, causing her to shift in her seat trying to back away from his obvious leer. "I'd be happy to put what's left over in a box."

My knees hit the tabletop as I stood up. "Hey asswipe, didn't your mother teach you to look a woman in the face when you speak to her?" The waiter backed up when he realized he was dealing with a predator's stare. Takes one to find one. That was my philosophy. I tossed my napkin onto the table and narrowed my eyes. "Any fucking idea who I am?"

Josh looked like a deer in headlights. "Whoa, man. Totally my bad. I'll get you both a beer on the house and that to-go box. I wasn't looking at her that way, I promise!" The waiter turned and fled.

"That was…weird. I've never had that happen before." She sounded sincere, but I imagined she turned the head of every man no matter what the venue.

"You're a great liar." I laughed. "And quite classy, Miss Wolfgram."

"I'm pretty sure my attire screams anything but classy."

Before I could suggest we blow this joint, both our phones erupted. Text after text coming in.

"Sorry," we both said at the same time. I checked my texts. Dane. With impeccable timing as usual.

Dude, you totally have to come to Snickers.

I'm hitting on the hottest chick right now and eavesdropping on some pastor or someone who's a hot mess. So much fun! Ditch your prude date and get down here. Now!

There was only one pastor in town that I knew of. Manda's brother. And if Dane was talking to him, that could only mean trouble.

Stay away from the pastor! I'll be right there.

I stuffed my phone back in my coat, and Manda's wide-eyed expression told me the news on her phone was no better than mine. Vito stopped by with the rest of our pizza in a box. "I'm so sorry, Mr. Sackes. Josh is no longer employed here."

I gave him a nod. I laid a few hundred on the table. "See that he gets what's left from the bill. He's a kid. He'll learn." The people I knew were as honorable as they were dishonorable.

"Ready to go?" I ushered Manda down the steps and into the crisp, night air.

"Actually, I'm sorry to cut this short, but I have to go deal with some family drama." She stuck out her hand to try to hail a cab.

I ushered her back onto the curb and stepped into the street to do the job myself. "Where are you going?" I unzipped my jacket and placed it over her shoulders. "You're shivering." The Chicago wind whipped around us and stung my cheeks. Our breaths came out in staccato puffs of smoke.

"Thanks for the coat, but my face is cold, too. Can you rip off those fake side burns and let me use them?" There was the cutest twinkle in her eyes.

"Nope, the Phantom never lifts his mask."

"Aren't we the secretive one?" She heaved a heavy sigh. "Look, I wasn't completely honest with you. My brother—the pastor—is hammered at Snickers, that gross bar by our building. His wife kicked him out after the church secretary caught him shopping for lingerie at work. Now my best friend Vanessa is drinking with him, and I'm afraid she'll only egg him on. I need to convince him to go home before he does something stupid, like drunk calls his wife."

A cab stopped for us, and I opened the door to let her slide in first. "I'm afraid I can't let a beautiful woman enter a seedy bar like that all by herself. We go in together, deal? I'll make sure you at least find your brother." No way was she going there alone; that much was for sure. Something about this girl made me want to tether myself to her and never let her out of my sight again.

Cars honked at the green light, but groups of happy Saturday night holiday revelers ignored the traffic signal and crossed the intersection with linked arms, singing and laughing. Snickers was the last place I wanted to go. It was Dane's favorite spot to pick up one-night stands. And if he was there talking to Manda's brother, I was sunk. Snickers was good for one thing: drinking yourself under the table then going home with a random stranger. Not my gig. I leaned forward to give the cabbie our address and added, "Can you hurry, please?"

"Look, I had a nice time, but you can go do whatever you want. You don't have to come with me and deal with my brother."

"No, let me come along. Maybe I can help. Besides, no way I'm letting you go into that dive without a bodyguard." I had another thought. "Call me," I instructed. "In case we get separated in the bar, I'll text you."

"Suit yourself, Wolverine Romeo."

I had a plan. Scan the bar for Dane and make a beeline for him. I had to get him out of there and corral my sibling before he shot off his mouth and ruined everything.

CHAPTER NINE

MANDA

"The fool doth think he is wise; but the wise man knows himself to be a fool."
(As You Like It 5.1.30-31)

I sat in the cab with Wolverine Romeo...who totally asked for my phone number!

Satisfied with the exchange of digits, he went back to staring out the window. Turned out he wasn't such a bad guy even though I wanted to rip off the fake side burns like nobody's business! The intensity when he looked at me over dinner made me want to whimper. Utterly demanding of my attention and infinite compassion tucked inside the sixth-floor hottie? Who knew?

After the waiter incident, I knew he had a wicked protective side. Avoiding all personal questions told me he had a secretive side. Too bad I was completely lost to his dead sexy side. I found myself giddy over the fact he was accompanying me to Snickers. I didn't want to let him go tonight. Or ever. I could be his new flask, and he could ditch the dirty magazines with me by his side.

Okay, I was an idiot and trying to rationalize my obsession with Dane.

Regardless, my family's issues were wackadoodle. And for tonight, I decided to trust him, as it seemed the sixth-floor hottie was fast turning into my protective knight. And I liked it. Who said chivalry was dead? He might have forgotten to hold the cab door open for me earlier in the day, but tonight, he had been nothing but a gentleman. The sad fact of continuing our date while hanging out my brother's dirty laundry wasn't my idea of fun, but what could I do?

Another text dinged as the cab slowed outside our condo. From my boss:

Sorry about Maggie. Find a ghostwriter for the series. It's your bread and butter. Sorry love, but it's dog-eat-dog in the literary world. Make sure you send the family a card. Sign it from the agency. What about the signing?

"What?" I exclaimed. I had to show Dane the text. "Can you believe this guy?"

Dane sniffed like it was no big surprise. "Money talks, remember. Your boss sounds like a dick. What are you going to do?"

"I have no idea." And that was completely the truth. "First thing first, I guess," I said with slumped shoulders and a new problem to cause me to toss and turn.

Dane paid the cabbie, offered me his hand to get out of the cab, and then held the door open to Snickers.

The stink of the disgusting dive assaulted me. Snicker's resembled Moe's out of the *Simpsons*. A long bar ran the length of the narrow establishment, and high, round tables with stools lined the opposite wall. A dartboard and jukebox sat near the front windows, and a sticky, scratched-up oak dance floor led to a single bathroom where I wouldn't be able to ignore the smell of dried urine and last night's vomit. The place was a hick townie bar severely out of place near the shopping mecca of Michigan Avenue.

"There he is." I pointed to Pete, who sat perched on a barstool by the front window. I could hear his voice over the barroom din while he waved his empty bottle at the bartender for a refill.

Dane wrapped an arm around my waist and pulled me close. "I'll be back. You talk to your brother, okay?"

Pete jumped up and pushed his way toward me. He looked happy to see me. Too happy. "Hey, Sis! Let's do a shot!" He banged on the bar to summon the bartender.

"I'm not here to do shots. I'm here to get you back upstairs. Dad said you left in a huff. Then Vanessa said you called her to come here for a drink. What the heck?"

Pete made his best frowny face. "I'm just having a little fun. Remember fun? We used to have it. Before Mom got sick and I had to be a person Sarah would be proud of all the time, not this guy." He poked a thumb into his chest. "Tequila. Dos, por favor."

He was right. We did used to have fun. In college, he'd take Vanessa and me out to parties where he made sure we went home together. We even road tripped to Florida one year for spring break. Before Mom was sick. Before he met Sarah. Before life changed us into sober adults. The tequila looked good. I grabbed the saltshaker, sprinkled some on my freshly licked hand, and did the old salt, drink, lime routine.

"I don't think what you did at work was technically wrong." I had to scream in his ear. "But drinking won't help. And I don't want you to do anything even dumber."

Pete pushed our shots out of the way and rested his elbows on the sticky bar top. "I won't. Hey, where is your date?"

"Yeah, he's over…" I looked, but didn't see Dane anywhere. Maybe he went to the bathroom. Or left. Looking around at all the scantily clad, makeup knowledgeable women around me, why would he want to hang out with me? Were these girls more his style?

"Go find him. I'm not going to do anything dumb. I just need to people watch and enjoy a few beers. Look, Vanessa went to the bathroom. She'll be right back. Go and don't worry about me. I need to contemplate if pretending to an entire congregation of people that I'm some perfect and pious pastor is really the right thing. Maybe this all happened for a reason. But I can't lose Sarah and Lily. I won't. Let me have a few with Vanessa, and I'll see you in the morning. Deal?"

I gave him the sisterly stare, squinting my eyes to see if he was telling the truth. He was. Vanessa pushed her way toward us and gave me a quick hug. "Where's your date?"

"I…he was just here." Still no sign of him.

Vanessa gave me a push. "Get out of here and find him! I've got the old Petey sitch. I owe him after all the times he took care of us."

"You're the best, Manda!" Pete yelled after me before turning back to chat with Vanessa and the new guy sitting next to them.

I walked to the back of the bar and waited by the men's bathroom. A guy who wasn't Dane came out. He wasn't here. He'd left me, and I didn't feel like telling Pete and Vanessa that my date was likely over. I decided to go home.

Twenty minutes later, there was a knock on my apartment door.

"Come in," I called, assuming Pete and Vanessa had finally had enough of the bar scene.

Wolverine Romeo.

"Thought you ditched me." I kicked off my shoes in the front hallway and struggled to uncork a bottle of Merlot in my pint-size kitchen.

"I'm sorry about that." He came up behind me and wrapped his arms around me. "Twist and push." He applied gentle pressure over my hand as we wove the corkscrew into the wine. With a loud pop, the cork gave way, and he released me.

I poured two glasses of wine, handed one to him, and padded over to the couch where I tucked my feet under my legs. He took a seat on the opposite end of the couch.

"How did you know my apartment number?"

"George."

Of course.

He raised his glass. "To no more interruptions."

Ditto, I thought. Our glasses clinked.

I felt pretty embarrassed about the whole day. "If you meant this to be a date, I'm sorry I'm out of practice. Crying my eyes out after your performance, then letting out family secrets before the third date."

"A lot of bad third dates then?" he joked.

If he only knew!

Beefer whined, and Dane scooched over to the far side of the couch so the dog could plop in between us. My traitorous canine moaned in satisfaction when Dane scratched his chin before I relocated him back to the floor. "To tell you the truth, I work so much that this is the first *first* date I've been on in a very long time."

I couldn't help but stare at him. Those crazy fake sideburns. The covetous looks he'd given Juliet on stage. I felt raw. Exposed. I wondered when actors knew to let their guards down. To stop being phony…scripted.

"You're looking at me..." he started. "Why? I know I'm ugly, but..."

My breath hitched. Was I turned on by Dane or the actor I saw on stage? "It's just how you stared at Juliet on stage."

He smiled. "Well, that was acting. And this isn't." Sliding toward me, he clasped a strand of hair between two fingers and touched it gently to my cheek. "I don't want to do anything to scare you away, Manda. I know I can be...a lot. I just want someone to get to know the real me."

"You can't scare me away," I said, entirely scared. I got that feeling—the butterflies in my stomach, heart in my throat, head dizzy feeling—of searing attraction. How was he so different than every other guy I'd ever met?

Releasing the lock of hair he'd been playing with, he cradled my face with his hand to pull me closer. And every cell of my body screamed for him not to stop.

Just as our lips were about to touch, my phone rang. My body gave an involuntary jerk that ruined the moment.

He pulled away.

"I'm not going to answer that," I insisted, leaning toward him again.

"I can wait, Manda. No rush, I'd rather have it be perfect. Do what you have to do."

Angry at my phone, I saw it wasn't a Pete emergency, but Ally. I slid the button to answer the call, mentally promising to be quick and then shut down my phone. "Hey, what's up?"

Ally was crying on the other line. "We got in a fight. I didn't know where to go. I'm downstairs, can you let me up?"

"Uh..." I looked at Dane, remembering what he'd said about wanting to be perfect. This was not perfect. "Sit tight. I'll be right down."

Dane gave a hearty laugh. "Now what? It seems tonight, it is simply not meant to be."

Dagnabbit! "My friend Ally got in a fight with her husband

and is crying in the lobby. Seriously, nothing ever happens to me, and today of all days, nothing will stop happening. I'm so sorry." I shouldn't be angry Ally called and needed me, but I was annoyed. Her timing was terrible. I hopped off the couch and deposited our wine glasses in the kitchen.

"I'll walk you down if you promise to let me take you out again."

"Deal." I reached out to shake his hand, but he grabbed me and pulled me close. Every hard muscle in his body felt like my home. For the first time in forever, I was actually looking forward to a second date. With no drama or interruptions!

Downstairs, Ally stood in the lobby, dabbing the corners of her wet eyes.

"Dane, this is my friend, Ally."

"Hi." He reached out to shake her hand, but she brushed him away.

"Oh no, I totally forgot about your date. *This* is the elevator man?" Ally said.

I bobbed my head up and down. "Vanessa can't keep anything a secret, can she?"

Dane stood taller like he was proud to be with me.

"I'm really sorry to bug you guys. I'll leave," Ally said.

"It's fine," Dane backed away from us. "I know where to find her."

Ally followed him, circling around him like a shark. "My-my, a chiseled jawbone under those sideburns?" Ally ran her fingers through his hair, making Dane visibly uncomfortable. "Gabriel Aubry hair." He shifted further away from her, likely beginning to question my taste in friends. Ally flashed me a pearly grin. "You're irresistibly gorgeous."

"Thanks?" Dane looked like a caged animal who wanted to escape.

"Oh, I wasn't talking to you, sunshine. I was talking to Manda."

I laughed. "My friends can be a tad…much."

Ally placed both hands on her hips, like a mother. "Listen here, playboy, if you think you're going to lure her to your bed and dump her, think again. Hurt her, and you have me to answer to. Got it?"

"Got it," Dane answered with a mock salute.

"Ally, stop!" My face and neck were on fire with embarrassment, and I gave Ally a horrified look, which sent my friend into a fit of laughter.

"Kidding!" She pointed a finger at him. "Mostly."

I grabbed Ally to pull her to the elevators. "Come upstairs, and we can sort out whatever you and Mark are fighting about."

"Thanks. I'm sorry I ruined your date," she whispered. "It was nice to meet you, Dane," she called over her shoulder and gave him a wave.

After pushing the up arrow, I ran back to Dane. Standing on my tiptoes, I whispered in his ear. "Sorry about Ally. She's a little…"

"I like her. Really. She seems quite protective of you."

"She helped me a lot after my mom died."

Wrapping his arms around me in a tight hug, he said, "I know from experience losing someone you love is devastating. And having someone like me around won't be any help. I had a great time tonight. See you around." Without a backward glance, he left through the revolving doors.

See you around? I told Ally about our quick goodnight. "He's never going to call me, is he, Ally?" I blew it.

Ally shrugged. "I don't know. He seems to like you."

Ally needed girl time to discuss everything as much as I did. My life changed in a day. A dead author. My job on the line. Pete and Sarah estranged. And worst of all, mixed signals from Wolverine Romeo. "We need ice cream, and it just so happens I have some.

CHAPTER TEN

HARRY

"Where having nothing, nothing can he lose."
(King Henry the Sixth Part III 3.3.152

Dane was pacing back and forth like a caged animal in the apartment, eating the leftover pizza. He did not appreciate being hauled out the back door of the bar and forced to go home via the service elevator.

"I told you. Right now we are *too* close." With Manda embroiled in her family issues, I'd caught Dane before Manda saw us. "You know we can't be seen in public together."

"So bring her up here and take me up on my offer of taking her for a test run to…you know, see if I approve." Dane waggled his eyebrows.

"She's not like that." I gave him no room for interpretation.

"They all are, Bro. Years in the human trafficking business and how many wanted to be saved?" Dane made a sad statement of fact. "They are lost by the time we get them."

"That's why we have to stop this from happening to them…sooner." We had a plan. Nothing would work if we didn't stick to the plan. "Manda is a pure-of-heart woman. Not someone who wants to jump in the sack with either one of us. She's a literary agent for crying out loud. How do you think my date would go if she saw…well, you know?"

"She'd bolt. Which is what I'm about ready to do. This life is killing both of us. If we don't get a break soon…" Dane's voice was pleading. "You could write legit. And maybe Manda is the answer. Give this all up. Have her take your career to the next level…if you know what I mean."

"Please!" I never begged Dane for anything. Ever. "Stick to the plan. Remember I still need to get a visual of the Cincinnati Bowtie. You were looking forward to that."

Dane's shoulders dropped, and I actually felt bad. Deep inside, this may all come to nothing, and we both knew it. "That's true," he conceded. "Keep your dirty little secrets from the prissy agent for now. But I want all the sordid details later, and I will be contemplating my price for this interruption in my soon-to-be-getting-laid evening. So why are you up here with me anyway?"

~

After the almost kiss and meeting Ally, I needed a cold shower, but a brisk walk would have to do. Manda's friend had redeemed herself with each syllable. I felt a sudden kinship with anyone who wanted to protect Manda and her sweet innocence. Step one to that end meant keeping her far away from me. Her warm eyes, fierce intelligence, and hot librarian look melted my gruff exterior. Was the sizzle of attraction I felt one-sided?

Not that it mattered. I wouldn't hurt her. This was our first and last date. Best to shut her out and keep her safe. Or that's what I told myself. I couldn't let anyone get too close. But

Manda's sincerity and innocence made me want to hold her in my arms and never let go.

Nothing I did erased Manda's beautiful face from my mind. I'd seen her sad, remorseful, embarrassed, and turned-on. And I'd memorized every detail. Even the soft curves of her body felt like a perfect match to mine. For the first time in forever, I would have looked forward to a second date.

Too bad that would never happen.

After grabbing a late-night coffee, I finally settled into bed with Desdemona. I figured Dane had gone to bed until I heard voices in the hallway a few moments later.

He must have gone back to Snickers to scoop up a few of his regulars. I turned up the volume to my headphones, hoping Dane would make it quick tonight. I wasn't in the mood.

About ten minutes later, I heard a woman screech and yell out, "What the fuck, Harry!" which made me crack open the bedroom door. Peering across the hall into my brother's bedroom, I caught too good a view of my brother fooling around with two naked girls.

"Were your balls in her mouth? Ick!" A third girl stood in the hallway watching, her back to Harry. Well, I guess that was my visual of the Cincinnati Bowtie. Not great.

Could my life get any weirder?

In answer to my own question, I looked left and caught a passing glance of Manda's brother, holding one of my books, walking into our kitchen!

"I told you I wanted to watch, but ew…" Hallway girl wobbled toward me, and I closed the door. "Pete, time to go!" she called.

Clad in boxers, Dane bounded out of his bedroom and rushed after them. "Wait up. What's the rush?"

"Good night, Harry. Thanks for the books." Pete hugged him tightly, the way drunks often do. "Call my sister on

Monday. Manda Wolfgram. She's an agent." The other girl kept moving.

Dane tugged at her. "Vanessa, wait."

It was like a scene from bad reality TV. I couldn't seem to tear my eyes away.

"That wasn't exactly what I had in mind when I said I wanted to be a voyeur. In fact, I'm pretty sure I've changed my mind about that idea. So you go about your"—she waved her hand toward the girls—"business. It's been interesting." She stuck out her hand to shake Dane's before thinking better of the idea. She whipped her hand away and turned to go.

"This is good stuff!" A thump from the hallway must have meant Pete had found a spot to read. "Chapter two," he announced, reading out loud from one of my books.

Would this evening never end?

"This isn't me. Not the real me. Give me another chance." Dane's voice sounded different. Stronger. More commanding than the twin who never cared to pick up his old pizza boxes. But would she get over the visual of his balls being dangled over another girl's mouth?

Unlikely.

"Maybe another time. C'mon, Pete. Time for night-night." They left out the front door and didn't even close it behind them.

I edged past Dane on my way to the front door, giving him a WTF look. Shrugging, he went back to his room. A *ding* and a *swoosh* from the hallway said the elevator opened on our floor. Behind me, the sound of moaning from Dane's room meant the trio was back at it. Two sets of heavy boots stomped down the hall, so I peeked out before closing the front door. Two uniformed policemen held up badges in front of Pete and Vanessa. The first officer sported a thick mustache and an impressive beer gut. He held up a meaty hand. "Are you Mr. Harry Sackes?"

"Nope, we're in 805. You're looking for 603." Vanessa never broke her stride. "Good-night, Harry!" She waved over her shoulder without looking back.

Pete giggled.

Shit.

The officers fast approached, and I had no time to shut the door. "Sir, we have reason to believe you have solicited prostitutes. Are they still on the premises?"

"Yes, sir. I did invite some friends to come up here and have a drink, but I had no knowledge the girls were hookers. Cross my heart." I made an X over my heart.

"Save it. We're taking you"—the cop pointed to me—"downtown. Get those girls out here."

I disappeared down the hallway toward Dane's bedroom where the three of them were busy and unaware of what was waiting in the hallway. When we returned, the officers cuffed the girls and me in the hallway.

One of the girls caught my sleeve. "When will Harry come bail us out?"

"I am Harry," I said.

She leaned in closer and examined the long scar that started by my right ear and ended at my jawline. "But that scar…"

I jerked away from her. "Shut up. You're getting paid good money to keep your mouths shut. I am Harry Sackes."

I only needed my one allotted phone call. But for now, I had to play nice.

CHAPTER ELEVEN

MANDA

"I do desire we may be better strangers."
(As You Like It 3.2.264)

I washed the bowls from last night's tear fest and ice cream extravaganza. After an hour, Ally had finally agreed to go home to Mark so they could kiss and make up. I snuggled in with Beefer to the sounds of horns honking, sirens wailing, and tires squealing before I drifted off to sleep amid the city's churlish lullaby, dreaming of a mash-up of Romeo on stage and Wolverine versus Waiter.

But an odd text from Vanessa left me rushing around to get up to Dad's condo and hear about the rest of Pete's night. Something about an erotica writer, hookers, and the fuzz. After our morning walk, I let myself in to Dad's condo. My father wasn't there, but I did find Pete out cold in the spare bedroom. He sounded like a bulldozer. How could Sarah put up with this snoring? The lingerie shopping seemed like it should be less important than this ruckus.

"Wake up!" I shook my brother, who didn't budge. I shook him harder.

Pete hiccupped, looked at me, and started giggling. "When did Vanessa leave?"

"I don't know. What in the world did you do in that icky bar for that long?" I thought of the amount of sticky beer on the floor and the clientele that valued Irish car bombs and painful footwear.

Pete rolled over and stretched before wobbling to a sitting position. "We hung out with the coolest guy who lives in your building, and he's an author! He invited us to his place." Pete nodded and giggled again like a thirteen-year-old boy before zigzagging his way to the living room couch. "Really nice guy."

Pete began humming an old Billie Joel tune I couldn't quite place.

Coffee was a necessity, so I put on a pot. Dad knew I came up here for the expensive dark roast beans we both loved. "I think you and Vanessa lost your ever-loving minds, big brother." I couldn't help but remember all the shenanigans the three of us got into in college.

"Oh shit." He fussed with his bed head. "I think someone got arrested. Almost forgot about that. But I haven't had that much fun in years. Hey, Sissy, this Harry guy is a good writer. You know, with your help—" He hiccupped, then held up a book with two women in bras kneeling before a Scotsman in a kilt.

"Arrested?" I picked up the book, refusing to even give it a cursory glance before tossing it posthaste into the trash. Quite sure there was nothing I could do to help that guy. "Oh, please. Good writer, huh? You're a moron, Pete." I handed him a cup of coffee. "Here, drink this."

He took a loud sip and sighed in content. "Manda?"

"Yeah?"

"Do you think I'm a bad person?"

"Of course not. You goofed up once. Sarah will get over it." I heard the key rattle in the lock, and Dad smiled at us drinking coffee curled up in his living room. "Save your old man a cup of joe? I bought us lunch." He set the paper bag down in the kitchen. He tossed Pete a Gatorade and an unopened pack of saltines. "See I'm not so old that I'm out of touch with how to cure a hangover!" We all laughed.

I took a whiff and immediately knew where the food came from. "Chicken from Crisp?"

Dad nodded. "To nosh on during the game. I can't remember the last time I've sat with Pete and watched a game.

He was right. Sarah was never far from his side. Not that it was a bad thing. But football games were a dry event with Pastor Pete and Stuffy Sarah. She always steered the conversation back to the congregation. It made me happy that for one afternoon, Dad had his only son there to drink a beer and watch football with him.

Like the old days.

"But first, Son, call your wife and apologize. You can't stay here forever."

Grabbing his phone, Pete headed down the hall. We both gave him a thumbs-up. I got three plates of food ready, which I set on the scuffed-up dining room table—the same table I grew up with, one of the few remnants of our suburban upbringing.

Pete returned too quickly. "No answer. It is *Sunday*. And the assistant pastor is taking over for me right now. I should have looked at the time. I'll try again later." While Dad was in the kitchen getting napkins and utensils, Pete leaned over and whispered, "Hanging out with Harry was a slamming good time. I'm telling you his writing really isn't half-bad, Sis. He could take off with the right agent."

"Please stop talking unless you have something useful to say. Maybe your drunk memory serves correctly and he was arrested last night. Then it sounds like he needs a lawyer, not an agent," I added with a laugh. "Besides, I can't represent *that* kind of writing. If I took on even one of those authors, they'd all be knocking on my door."

The moment Dad sat back down, Pete launched into the story. "Want to hear about my night?"

"Why, is it all coming back to you now?" I loved harassing my brother. It had been so long. I usually kept my mouth shut around Sarah so as not to garnish a disapproving look.

"You said you needed some air," Dad said. "I thought you went for a walk. Hey, Manda, I almost forgot. How did your date go?"

"It might have been better if I hadn't gotten a call that Maggie Monroe died."

Dad put his arm around me. "That's terrible. What happened?"

I told them about her sudden death and missing the news of her book's success and now Roger wanting me to find a ghostwriter. "So the date was fine I guess, but my mind was preoccupied." And no first kiss.

"So let's get to the fun part of the night," Pete piped up, trying to lighten the situation. "I did go out for air. Then I ended up at Snickers and met this cool writer who lives in the building. I even got a signed copy of one of his books."

"That I've already thrown in the garbage!" I added.

Dad looked in the garbage can and spit out some coffee when he saw the cover. "Good grief, Pete. That would only happen to you!" Not missing a beat, Dad went back to the fridge, snatched up two beers, cracked them open, and set one down in front of Pete. "That'll help your hangover more than a sports drink." He pulled up a chair at the kitchen table, rested his elbows on the table, and took a smooth draw on his own beverage. "Glad you're finally back, Son. It's time you realized God won't send anyone to hell for drinking a beer. Now, have one with your old man and continue to tell me more about all the good decisions you're making."

"I never said—"

"Pete, I swear I refuse to have this water-into-wine argument with you again. Have a beer with your old man. It won't kill you." Dad laughed when Pete made a face. After the previous night, he was back to thinking alcohol was poison.

Ah, the joys of watching someone nurse a hangover. "He's teasing," I mouthed.

Pete shook his head, unable to conceal his smirk and tipped his own beer back. "Sarah's family would be mortified at my behavior." While Dad fiddled with the TV to find the game, Pete leaned toward me. "Probably more so about the hookers than the beer."

"Hookers?" I whispered.

"Son, pardon my French, but who the hell cares? I'm not saying get drunk every night or that being a dumb ass is fine. Just…you know, be yourself. Manda, what's that saying you like?" He snapped his fingers, trying to remember.

"'To thine own self be true.'" *Hamlet*. Dane would be incredible as Hamlet. Back in those baggy pants, the sword fighting, the tortured expression he'd wear over Ophelia's death. I shifted in my chair. I wanted to see him on stage again. My own private stage.

"That's all I'm saying. Don't try to be somethin' you're not for anybody. Sarah fell in love with you before you were converted. Talk to her, and work it out."

After the game, I went back up to my place and let my lazy afternoon thoughts drift back to Dane. Beefer needed his long walk, and then I crawled back into bed with my laptop to do some work.

The world had all kinds of people. Trained Shakespearian actors. Erotica authors like this Harry from my building. And I crossed my fingers that Dane would get another chance…

soon…at a real first kiss. One like you read about in the greatest love stories.

I opened some query emails. The third one stopped me cold:

Dear Hottie McAgent Wolfie, aka my Manda,

It was such a pleasure meeting your brother this weekend and letting him peruse my work firsthand. I think I'm finally ready to take my writing to the next level, and you, my dear, are my girl. Don't pass me off to another agent. My answer will be no. But if you sign me, I'll take you to heights you never thought possible.

Yours,
Harry Sackes

Something about that name jogged my memory. I pulled out the program for *Romeo and Juliet*. The playbill read, "Romeo…played by *Dane Sackes.*"

Please no. Don't let them be related.

CHAPTER TWELVE

HARRY

"The better part of valour is discretion;"
(King Henry the Fourth Part I 5.4.120)

The local precinct was like any other in city limits. I should know; I'd acquainted myself with quite a few of them. I had a bad habit of getting into trouble, part of what started me down this road to recovery a long time ago.

After promising the girls some extra cash if they kept their traps shut, all I had to do was wait for my phone call. I was booked, fingerprinted, and they took my picture. I smirked, showing my good side. Only then did I get my phone call. He answered on the second ring.

"It's Harry. I'm in the clink with some girlfriends. A little help?"

"Someone will come."

I had clean and dirty connections in the city. Vito was dirty. He worked with the street girls and played false rat for the cops. He knew my predilections to having the youngest girls he had. To keep poking the bee's nest, I needed a rap sheet. It looked good for what I was trying to do. Find the traffickers. Not the small players. I was after the big guys. The guys who snatched runaways and dumped them on a ship to never-come-home land. The seedy world of human trafficking. I was trusted to pay good money for girls…mostly ones that Dane had fun with. I had a good reputation for not hurting them, and no one ever saw Dane or me in the same place. That's how we made it work.

The handcuffs were cutting off my circulation, so I was glad when the arresting cop removed them and pushed me inside a room for questioning. "I'd love some coffee, please. Four sugars, two creams."

"You'll get it black if you get it at all." A snarky fellow. I didn't care for his attitude.

No coffee and no nobody for an hour.

Then the doorknob turned, and there was a plainclothes guy with Styrofoam cups. Good, 'cause I'd had a long day and dawn was a few hours away. "About time." I hadn't meant to bark at him, but it came out that way.

He looked me up and down and shook his head. He must have been a fed. "Word is you took a girl out on a legit date. She ditch you already? Or she see the cover of your last book?" Although I'd never seen this guy before, he obviously knew who I was.

"It was a business date, and she picked the restaurant. I just didn't feel like waiting. And as it so happens, the date went south and I went back to old habits. They die hard, so I hear."

He took off his glasses and wiped them on his shirt before taking a seat across from me. "So, we got a tip. Shipment going out soon with local girls—young—and they are looking to grab as many more as they can in the next week. A man they call The Giant is paying cash at the drop a week from Monday. I don't have any more details than that. But I'm going to send word up that you'll like a few hours with a fresh pick before they ship off. You'll have to pony up the cash."

This was the break I'd hoped for. All these long years. What everyone didn't know was my plan was to kill every sick bastard my gun could reach. If I died in the process, so be it. Maybe I could finally rest in my small piece of retribution. "How much?"

"Offer 10K an hour."

"Done." The words were out of my mouth so fast even the fed gave me a nod of astonishment.

"Lucrative career or something?"

"Or something," I answered.

I was "transferred" to his custody after he made it a federal thing. I made him take the girls, too. He dropped us off at a local diner and told the girls, "Aren't you lucky Harry is rich and paid his way out of this?" The girls looked grateful and hungry, so I bought them food. Sue me. Dane was once again pacing the apartment when I got home in the late afternoon on Sunday.

"Where the hell have you been?" Dane charged me as soon as I came through the door. Desdemona wagged her tail but didn't move from the couch. "I didn't know who I could call. Did you need bail? What about the girls? And who's the narc? I'm thinking it's that new bartender. I hadn't seen him before last night. I'm calling the owner. We need to get out of this. Run. Hide. Reinvent ourselves. You can publish the great American novel, and I'll act for local Shakespeare companies. What about Portland? Let's move to Portland."

I placed both hands on his shoulders. "Shh." Once he quieted, I said, "We have a tip. A good one. Might be all we need. Understand?"

Dane took a deep breath and went out on the balcony to have a cigarette. Years had passed since I'd seen him smoke. Poor guy must have been really worked up. But the less he knew, the better. He just needed to maintain my Harry Sackes street cred as a horny erotica author. It worked.

"How did the rest of your date go?"

I hated to admit it, but I had to call it. "It was a bust. What possessed you to bring her damn brother up here?"

"He latched onto me. Not my fault! And the hot girl kept saying how she wanted to watch so she didn't consider it cheating on her boyfriend. I don't know. I got carried away. And then I signed your books and gave him a copy. Like I said, if you land an agent, maybe we can walk away from this."

Poor Dane. He didn't know how far into the pit I'd fallen with these people. The good ones like Vito. The bad ones I'd been begging for younger and younger girls hoping for this kind of chance. And now here it was. I should be happy.

But I only felt nauseous.

I opened my computer and did something I was sure I'd regret. I sent Manda flowers.

My days could be numbered a week from tomorrow. Maybe I could give the woman, who would never be mine, some small measure of happiness.

CHAPTER THIRTEEN

MANDA

> *"that which we call a rose*
> *By any other name would smell as sweet;"*
> *(Romeo and Juliet 2.1.85-86)*

Monday Morning

Working my way toward my office the next morning, I juggled my coffee, computer bag, and oversized purse. Tossing down my stuff, I almost tipped over the two dozen roses on my already overcrowded desk. Assaulted by the sweet scent, I moved my computer bag and purse onto the floor and set the coffee on a side table piled high with books, manuscripts, and Maggie's latest shipment of books and promotional materials like bookmarks, postcards, and banners.

Flowers?

My office was not much bigger than Vanessa's walk-in closet. My desk had space for my computer, a lamp with a red velvet shade, piles of paper edits, and my beloved hover drone remote control toy. Impossible to keep the tiny space tidy, I'd resigned myself to overcrowded bookshelves and endless stacks of paper. My one indulgence being a matching red velvet reading chair placed adjacent to the prison-sized window, which boasted a view of yet another high-rise. But light of day was light of day.

With both hands finally free, I collected a bunch of the roses, still in petite bud form, and held them to my face, like a mother holds a child's face before smothering it in kisses. Closing my eyes, I inhaled deeply as the silky buds tickled my fingertips. A note was attached, the envelope inscribed with the insignia of a florist two blocks east of this building.

I plopped into my reading chair by the window and ripped open the envelope, savoring the fact the words inside were written in messy cursive. A handwritten note was fast becoming a lost art with the advent of email and flowers dot com.

Dear Manda,

What's in a name? I'd never judge you by yours and hope you don't judge me by mine. I'd like another chance to show you who I am, if you'll let me. I can still feel you in my arms after R&J.
Dane

Holy schnickes. Finding it hard not to be smitten, I shot Ally a text:

Dane sent roses. I guess a second date is a go!

He *wasn't* this hooker-loving Harry Sackes fellow! And he wasn't in jail! Maybe, like me, he would be aghast at the surname similitude that resides in our otherwise cool building. I let out a sigh of relief and got to work, singing a tune and letting the rose scent waft into the hallway.

Every time I tried to concentrate on work, my mind drifted

back to Dane. Like I was writing a scene description of a character. The crooked tip of his nose. The sideburns I was sure to rip right off if he donned them on our next outing. Strong shoulders that propelled him forward with the graceful gait of a practiced knight. Ally got to tousle his wavy, dark blond hair with her fingers. No fair! I'd cast him in stone and set him in my apartment as a decorative Greek statue next to a bookshelf.

"Who dropped those flowers off this morning?" Roger Peddet loomed in the doorway, snapping me out of my alternate universe of crazy. His form was a marked contrast to the sunny window and budding roses. As usual, my boss's mere presence jerked me back to reality. With his pressed suit and a full head of silver hair that flouted his age, I swore the man could sell stink to a skunk. He had a way of making you feel like his way was the only right way and any attempt to dissuade or dissent was considered a preposterous act of treason.

Well-known in New York, he'd moved to Chicago and set up shop three years ago so his wife could be closer to her aging parents. With all his kids out of the house and his wife being almost a full-time caregiver, the man lived, ate, and breathed literature. No one would argue he knew his stuff. He could anticipate the market with frightening accuracy.

"A delivery guy?" I slid aside the picture of my father and me at a Cub's game to make room for the vase.

Roger grunted, satisfied with my cavalier response that was really no response at all. "Did you send that card to Maggie's husband? It was nice of your dad to send flowers to brighten your mood."

Good, he thinks my dad sent the flowers.

If Roger thought I had a boyfriend, he'd fret over my time constraints. He wanted me working, reading, and editing. No time was allowed for any level of fun or, God forbid, fornication.

He clapped once like he did when starting a motivational

speech for aspiring authors. "Now, you need to get your head back in the game. We just got the go ahead for her book signing. How about you dress up and pretend to be a princess? That'll work." His tone was hollow and unsympathetic, caring only about his bottom line. Not my grief.

Another deliveryman, dressed head to toe in brown with a small cap and orthopedic shoes, came into view behind Roger. Carrying an envelope, he snapped his gum and referred to an electronic device in his right hand. "Package for a Ms. Wolfgram."

"That's me." I hopped up and signed for the envelope. Now that I was closer to him, I looked for a USPS, UPS, or FedEx badge. None. "Who do you work for?"

"I'm a private courier; our company ships only the most expensive items. You must have been on pins and needles waiting for this gold mine."

Roger and I exchanged a glance.

After the courier left, I ripped open the package and sifted through the pages.

"Well?" Roger tried to read over my shoulder.

"It's a cupcake recipe with a lot of lawyer mumbo jumbo at the end. I think Maggie bought this from someone, intending to…open up a cupcake shop or something."

The phone rang, and Roger took the sheets out of my hands to further peruse the documents. "Manda Wolfgram," I answered.

"Ms. Wolfgram, this is Taylor Monroe, Maggie's husband."

"I'm so sorry about your wife, Mr. Monroe." I covered the receiver and mouthed the words "Maggie's husband" to Roger. "I'm hoping to make it up to the service this week—"

"That isn't necessary. I called because I need your help with something else. Have you by chance received any kind of package Maggie had delivered to you by courier?"

"Yes, I have it here. It seems to be some kind of recipe."

"A recipe she paid thousands of dollars for along with signing a lease for a storefront! Can you find any way to use it with her books? Or the kids and I will go bankrupt. Maggie pulled money from our second mortgage. Now, after funeral expenses and what not, we're broke."

I took a moment to process what he'd said. "I'm not sure I understand."

"She had some crazy dream of a store where little girls can come in and be all old-school. Cook cupcakes with their parents, be treated like princesses—maybe even have a tea party. She begged me all the time. I told her no. She did all this without telling me, counting on the success of her books." His voice broke. "And now she's gone. What should I do? I'm grieving, but at the same time I'm so mad at her."

"I'd been trying to get a hold of her. She broke into the *New York Times* Children's Best Sellers List last week. Can you believe it? Now I have hundreds of her books, a huge book signing one week from today, and no more Maggie. Of course you'll continue to receive royalties, but it won't cover this. Not by a long shot. And if the series doesn't continue…"

With a few deep sighs, he collected himself. "Look, let me dig through her files a bit. I think she said she was almost done with the next one. Can't you have another author finish it? I'll forward you any files I find." Desperation seeped into every word. "Please say you can help. Maggie trusted you. Can I count on you?"

My heart sank, and I swiped at my damp eyes. What should I say? The truth was brutal: *Without Maggie, there are no more books.*

The man would crumble.

Roger helped himself to a seat at my desk and clicked something on my laptop.

"If you send me what you can find, I'll see what I can do."

What am I saying? I'll do my best to help you continue a series from a dead author?

"Thank you! I guess Maggie was right to trust you. I don't care how you keep her series going, but please try, because without that income..." He didn't have to continue. "Goodbye."

I clicked the phone shut and slumped in the red velvet reading chair to stare out the window. How was I supposed to come to terms with the complete and utter mess I'd landed myself in?

Roger's expression changed as his eyes scanned my laptop. What the heck? Why was my boss entranced by the computer screen? Then a slow, sly smile slid across his face. "Well, well, well...what do we have here?"

"Roger, I'll forward you a thousand crummy query letters later you can laugh at. Right now, I have an issue with Maggie. That recipe—she paid a bundle for it, and her husband wants to know if we can get another author to keep writing the *Pink Cupcake Princess* series. He needs the money."

My boss never lifted his head. "Sure, I already said you should have another one of your authors ghostwrite the books. And you go to the signing in a princess dress. No sweat." He cleared his throat and pushed up his glasses with a naughty smile still curling the corners of his lips. "Why didn't you tell me about your weekend?" He waggled his eyebrows.

"What are you talking about?" I moved to my computer, wondering what private email he'd intercepted.

"This guy? You can't possibly want—"

"Sign him." From Roger's tone it was not a suggestion.

"No!"

"Yes! Harry is the hottest indie erotica author out there. You sly dog. Why didn't you tell me you knew him? He'll make us both rich in a month. Email him our contract right now before he goes forward with another agency." Roger stood up like it was a done deal.

"He's a pig. I don't want to rep erotica. I agent children's books and literary fiction. I…I won't do it." I crossed my arms and stomped my foot in defiance.

Roger let the smile recede and replaced it with his salesman voice. "Maggie was your only money maker, right? Without her, I have dozens of interns who'd love your job." He put his arm around me in a fatherly way. "Take on Harry until you figure out who is going to ghostwrite Maggie's books. Then I'll take him on, personally, and you'll be done with him. He's a *gold mine*." He led me to the front desk, his hand still firm on my shoulder and me with my arms still stubbornly crossed. The thought of having to deal with this Harry guy on a regular basis made my skin crawl. And he lived in my building!

Roger turned to enunciate to our receptionist, Cindy. "Please get a contract ready for Manda and an author named Harry Sackes. That's S-a-c-k-e-s." He turned me to face him, squeezing both of my shoulders gently. "What do you say?"

Cindy giggled. "Wow, a real star. I've read *all* his books!"

I needed to make a choice.

CHAPTER FOURTEEN

HARRY

*"When sorrows come, they come not single spies,
But in battalions!"
(Hamlet 4.5.77-78)*

"Why are you chortling?" I asked my twin after I hung up with the Chinese restaurant I love for takeout. "What's up with you anyway? It's Monday. Aren't you supposed to be heading off to some froufrou play rehearsal?"

"Oh, I'm going. Just waiting around here to see if anything exciting happens."

I was pretty sure the weekend had been exciting enough, especially his night in jail. It put the "f" in fun. "Like what?"

"Any word from your literary love?"

I shook my head but refused to take my eyes off of him. Something was up. I could tell…the twin thing and all. He had been in an odd haze since he'd met Manda's friend Vannessa-the-Voyeur. I needed to kibosh any ideas he was entreating about double dates.

"Any word from the trepidatious voyeur who thinks you're me and among the dregs of society because you pen erotica?"

"Nope, and now I do have to go. Check your email, will you?"

Oh no. "Why? What did you do?" I raced to block the door, but he zipped out before I could corner him for interrogation. *Check my email?*

I drummed my fingers on the countertop, tunneling my vision to the small space visible through the patio doors that wasn't covered by blackout curtains, effectively ignoring all clutter between me and the sliver of life existing outside the apartment. I loved the anonymity the city afforded me. Innumerable takeout options, unlimited television and movie access via my computer and cable, and I had racked up a nice collection of shit from Amazon during late night shopping sprees.

All of which met my basic needs of food, clothing, and shelter, but something tugged at the back of my mind. I didn't need more of anything fake. I needed more Manda. But how? She was the something innocent and beautiful I'd spent years in telephone therapy trying to deny exists—the gentle virtue of girls.

Manda's friend Vanessa was not innocent. *Damnit. When I start thinking like scum, I become like them.* I opened a cabinet and poured a glass of Powers. A little early in the morning, but what did it matter? *I had broken my own rule: never let anyone in.*

My high walls built a lovely fortress. If I stayed in the protective turret, I could keep everyone around me safe. To rarely venture out or stray further than Snickers. I was the black plague on my own life. No one thought to institutionalize me after everything that happened, so I did it to myself.

Imprison myself from the world and the people in it that I could hurt or could hurt me.

My thoughts strayed back to Manda. Delicate. The naive

look in her eyes the other night brought back memories, horrific, painful memories that I'd successfully buried for years.

Damn you, Harry!

And yet, I was antsy today, unsettled and fidgeting…

Check the email. But something stopped me. Like there was bad news inside and I wasn't ready to read it. Even though Manda brought out the part of me that wanted—no, *needed* to reemerge, reengage, and even change. But it was too far gone.

No end to this life. No second chances to reinvent myself and start over. Not possible.

I already possessed the invisible stardom of authors: the ability to have anonymity so I could go anywhere and have no one know who the hell I was. Too bad I didn't go anywhere good. I had pretty boy Dane for the rare public appearances I did agree to.

I awoke from my waking slumber when the buzzer rang. George's familiar voice echoed through the holes in the plastic intercom. "Harry, your food's here. Can I send him up?"

"You know it, Georgie."

I peeled off a twenty from my cash stash and opened the door to the apartment. Walt Disney got one thing right; it sure as hell was a damn world of tears, hopes, and fears—at least to me.

At the elevator, I met the delivery guy. We exchanged nourishment for payment. Back in the apartment, I unwrapped the white paperboard oyster pails and carefully let the sides down to use as a plate. Chucking the complementary chopsticks into the garbage, I opted for a fork. Before even tasting it, I spritzed the chicken fried rice with a generous helping of soy sauce. Too lazy to remove the clutter on our three barstools, I ate standing up and contemplating…well, everything.

The phone rang. Damn, that therapist was punctual.

"Porn central. How can I get you off?" I licked my fingers.

"Hello, Harry. This is Doctor Lindstrom. How are you today?"

I swallowed before answering. "Good, you?"

"I'm fine. What's happened in your life since last week?" The therapist's monotone voice grated on me every time he called, as if you could only speak to crazy people in one pitch.

"Same old, same old. Hit up Snicks on Saturday and banged two gorgeous babes. They loved it, duh."

"Uh-huh." I heard a pen scratch. He was supposed to be taking notes on our interview for my patient records, but I wondered how often the good doctor just doodled or did a crossword puzzle, interjecting at the appropriate times with some unintelligible murmur to keep me talking.

But I did keep talking. I had to. Part of the contract with our mother to live with Dane in the city and not get moved to a group home in Bumblefuck, Illinois with shitty takeout. Everyone was always "worried" about me. I was considered "unstable."

Yup. Everyone was about to find out how right they were.

"Someone did show up and spoil my fun, though. Dane was on a date," I lied, twisting the truth into a one-eighty. "I got his date's pastor brother and hot bestie up to my place. She got an eyeful of my generous package and stellar technique."

"What happened then?"

"Dane got pissed, probably 'cause the girl was dripping just wishing she could get in the fray with me."

"You really think this girl wanted to join you?"

I took another bite of food, conscious to chew loudly into the receiver to annoy the good doctor. "Who wouldn't?"

"Harry, not all little girls grow up into the bar sluts you choose to associate with every weekend."

"Yes, they do!" I shouted. My heart raced, and the phone slipped from my ear due to the sweat coursing down my palm. "Women are all the same—complete wastes and good for only one thing." Chunks of rice flew out of my mouth and back onto the mock dinner plate.

"What's the woman's name, the one that walked in on you?"

"Manda." The name rolled off my tongue too easily. Like crème brûlée to the vocal cords. "Oh, and Dane's prissy date is a literary agent. I'm thinking about sending her a query email. We'd both get rich if she signed me. Plus, I'd probably get in her pants with all the money I'd make for her. Win-win with twin-twins."

The doctor continued to scribble. "Interesting. Besides your writing, blogging, eating, and sexual behavior patterns, which have remained stagnant for years, this is the first time I've heard you express a desire to change anything about your life."

"Maybe I *do* want to get to know Manda better, just to prove my point to Dane that all women are dumb sluts."

"Do you think your sister would have grown up to be a 'dumb slut' as you put it?"

"Session's over, asshole. You know the rules." I snapped the phone shut, my hands shaking so violently I couldn't bring the fork to my mouth. "Shit!" I yelled, launching the phone across the room. I grabbed the bottle of Powers, left the half-eaten food, and headed for the shower.

I turned the faucet to hot, stripped naked, and climbed into the tub with the booze. I sat in the back of the tub and drank while the water burned my feet.

When would the memories wash away?

I made myself a promise. One way or another, I'd end this. In one week.

CHAPTER FIFTEEN

MANDA

"And oftentimes excusing of a fault
Doth make the fault the worse by the excuse,"
(King John 4.2.30-31)

I knew a literary agent needed to be adaptive. Change with the times. But nowhere in the history of my aspirations did I ever consider repping erotica. Heck, I'd never even read the stuff.

My mind swam with rapid-fire thoughts, crisscrossing and examining all my options:

Not rep Harry: Maybe lose my job or get demoted.

Offer to rep Harry, and he refuses: Keeps boss happy.

Offer to rep Harry, and he agrees: Uh-oh SpaghettiOs. Roger gets his precious client and a windfall of money. Harry is stuck in my life for the next few months.

What about the *Pink Cupcake Princess* series? Who could ghostwrite it? The last thing I wanted to do was let Maggie's family down in their time of need. If her husband could find the next work in progress and I hired a ghostwriter...

That's it!

"I'll only take on Harry if he agrees to ghostwrite the end of Maggie's next book."

So irrational! Implausible!

I suppressed a smile.

Roger tapped his toes. "What about Calvin Forbes? Couldn't he finish the series?"

"He's on submission with Del Rey, is a lifelong bachelor, and wouldn't have a clue what to say to a child if one sneezed and asked him for a Kleenex."

"Okay, how about Jason Vandy? He's got kids."

I laughed out loud. "Right, he's got four boys, the youngest of whom is a sophomore in college. He couldn't write for little girls any more than Pete Koontz. Plus, he wants to genre jump from litfic to horror and keeps sending me pen name ideas and proposals."

"Who else do you have?"

"Lois Schaefer, who is a mother to girls but hasn't written a word for me since her writer's block hit eighteen months ago."

"All right. You could use Bryce Biele."

"Bryce is a rich man now because of us, and when his last book went on submission, he decided to take a hiatus to the Bahamas for the next blustery six months. He doesn't have a phone or computer there. Shall we go on?" I let a smile curl my lips. "Harry is my only option; it'll be a stipulation he finish the book in the next, say…two weeks, or I can break the contract. He's my best bet. He writes love stories anyway. The *Pink Cupcake Princess* series is just a clean love story for little girls. He clearly knows exactly what women want to read, so I'm sure he'll be the perfect match to writing for Maggie's audience, too."

"Fine." Roger called my bluff. "Send him the contract. If he declines you, tell him I'd prefer to rep him myself, even though he seems to be asking for you." Roger turned and headed toward his office, but after a few steps, he swung around. "I realize you like to maintain the whole Goodie Two-shoes persona, but if you don't get with the times, you'll become obsolete." He slammed the door to his office.

"Hmmph." I sniffed.

Cindy feverishly typed the entire time and pretended she wasn't listening. "Just to let you know," she spoke in co-conspirator kind of voice, "Harry is incredibly talented, and speaking as one of his biggest fans, he'd do amazing job with Maggie's books. I'm sure of it!" Cindy's eyes twinkled with fangirl excitement. "Do you think he'll come here to the office? I heard he's as hot as the heroes he writes. Plus, his books are always on sale for ninety-nine cents."

Cheap thrills. Good old Harry. *You've duped my own brother and my secretary. But I won't let you dupe me!* "Ninety-nine cents is wonderful. What would my cut of that be? Six cents?" I twirled my index finger in a circle. "Yippie."

Cindy hit "print." I snatched the contract and headed for the office to fume. *Why does Harry want me anyway? Maybe this is all one big joke.* I handwrote in the clause about ghostwriting the children's series "indefinitely" and walked it back to Cindy.

I wished I could see Harry's reaction to that one!

He'd never agree to this, would he?

Most likely, I was completely safe.

Before lunch, Cindy had the contract ready with my revisions and I wrote Harry a congratulatory email, with the given provisions of him being Maggie's ghostwriter.

I hit "send."

The whole while, the perfume of Dane's roses hung heavily in the air around me.

∾

"Let me know when you get a response from Harry." Roger loomed once again in the doorway to my office. The late-afternoon sun reflected off his bald head.

My day had been spent sifting through queries and editing manuscripts. My eyes hurt, and the pressure from Roger was making me ornery.

Every hour the guy had checked in to see if Harry had responded. The last time Roger was this jumpy was when one of his authors was nominated for the Noble Prize in Literature.

"I promise I will let you know the minute I hear from him." I was relieved I put the ghostwriting addendum in the contract. The guy would never accept that clause. "By the way, Maggie's husband found her manuscript for the next book. It's about half done."

"Workable?"

"It's a start. Needs a heavy edit and a great ending."

Roger chewed his lip. "I'm taking a gamble on you here, young lady. I'll stick my neck out and call Maggie's publisher. Tell him we'll have the manuscript ready very soon. You find me someone to finish that second book pronto, and I promise you a blowout book signing next Monday."

I kept my breathing steady. "A book signing with no author? Where your great idea is for me to dress up as a princess? You can't be serious."

"Now is the time to capitalize on her best-seller status. It would mean tons of sales, the name of the book getting out there, and money in the bank for Maggie's husband. So make it happen." He lumbered down the hall to harass the other agents.

I exhaled and dug in to really read the bones of Maggie's new book. It needed a lot of work and fast. Figuring Harry would be a dead duck, I emailed my other clients, begging for the last-minute help that would make or break my agency career.

Shoot! A bad girlfriend in the making, I hadn't even stopped to call Dane and say thank you for the flowers. Refusing to stoop to texting him, I found him in my contacts. Good thing we'd exchanged phone numbers in the cab on the way to Snicker's.

Voice mail.

"Dane, our date ended too soon. My desire is to see you anon." *I'm a dork.* I went to push "end" but stopped. "This is Manda by the way. Did you know there is another "Sackes" in our building? By the way, the flowers are gorgeous. Thanks."

Buffoon. I sound like an idiot.

Slipping my phone back into my purse, the light in my office changed yet again. Roger was back and with a smirk on his chubby face that I didn't like. He cleared his throat. "By the way, I need you to go in my stead to the writers conference on Wednesday and take pitches. Something else came up."

There was no arguing with the boss man. He booked himself for a least one conference a month to meet prospective authors and take their in-person pitches, but when the location was subpar, he pawned it off on the rest of his staff. "Where is it?"

"Skokie. You can drive."

"What's the conference?"

"I'll email you the details. I'm sure you'll have a blast." He left.

Conferences were never a blast. Hobnobbing with aspiring authors, pretending to laugh at their jokes, and calming their nerves was exhausting. At least the conference was local, so I wouldn't be expected to hang out at the bar and drink wine with conference coordinators. I could be home and snuggled into my own bed that same night.

Google popped up a list of upcoming writers conferences.

Only one in Skokie.

So that was why smirky Roger hadn't been forthright. The EAA conference.

Erotic Author's Association.

And who was the guest speaker? None other than Mr. Harry Sackes.

Splendid.

CHAPTER SIXTEEN

HARRY

*"...for there is nothing
either good or bad, but thinking makes it so:"
(Hamlet 2.2.251-52)*

"Harry, you home?"

I knew the apartment was dark, but I couldn't answer. Couldn't feel. Light appeared from beneath the bathroom door. I heard rustling in the kitchen. Dane must have found the leftover Chinese food. A bang on the bathroom door. "Hurry up, man. I gotta whiz."

More rustling and then the apartment door opened and closed. Maybe he took out the garbage, depositing it in the chute across the hall. The dog barked. Desdemona knew I was in here. Knew something was wrong.

I listened, wondering if I could pinpoint Dane's every move. Keys hung on the hook by the front door. Change and wallet emptied on his dresser. "Des, get off my bed," I heard him say. Four paws hit the ground. Dane probably smoothed out his navy comforter and then invited her back up on the bed. The flick of another light, maybe in his bedroom. Then he read lines out loud.

"I'm serious, Harry. Get a move on!" He rapped on the bathroom door again. I still didn't answer. He knew I was in here, door unlocked, scalding my skin.

"Harry?" He carefully opened the door. "You okay, man?"

The past haunted me. It had a tight hold on my psyche, and today I'd lost the battle for sanity. My feet were red-hot from the water. A few more minutes and I'd be covered in blisters. And I didn't give one shit.

"What's the matter?" he asked.

I was a mess. A failure. Numb to the present and lost to the past.

"What happened?" Dane placed his hands on my shoulders and gave me a gentle shake so I'd look him in the eye. I refused.

"Bad therapy session? I'll grab the Silvadene, yeah?"

Cabinet doors opened and closed in the kitchen. Dane was always prepared with a tub of the burn ointment for my bad days. He tossed gauze and paper tape on the bathroom counter, and I had a vague idea that he helped me out of the tub, dripping wet. He helped me into my robe and led me to the bed where I was able to lie down. I could hear everything happening around me, and I was not combative but compliant. It was just that I couldn't see anything from my current reality. I was reliving the past. Dane made sure the bedcovers didn't touch my feet. A chair squeaked at the end of my bed. My twin began to dress the burns. We said nothing to each other. I stared at the ceiling. The pain of the past always stronger than any pain I could inflict on myself in the present.

"You want to talk about it?"

I was silent.

"Did Manda get her roses today?"

My foot jerked when he dabbed the ointment on a particularly large well-formed blister.

"You should ask her out again."

"She's a closet slut like every other girl on the planet." I spoke the words, but they were not my own. I had to purge her from my mind. I would ruin her life.

It was Dane's turn to keep quiet. He taped the gauze over my feet, retrieved two pain pills from the medicine cabinet, and filled a small glass with tap water. He pressed the pills in my palm and helped me with the cup. "Take these. Tomorrow will be better."

I popped the pills and gulped them down with a splash of water. Dane set the water on the nightstand and flipped off the lights. "Why can't I burn away memories as easily as I can burn my feet?" The images flashed in my mind like a movie clip forever on replay. Our sister, Julie, laughing and trying to beat me home. The car door opening. Her screaming. The knife sliding across my face when I reached them. Me chasing the car until my legs gave out.

"Harry, it wasn't your fault. If I hadn't been sick that day..." He let his words hang in the air. The door shut.

Tuesday

The pain pills, booze, and shitty night's sleep did nothing to improve my mood the next morning. That was...until I opened my inbox.

Dane was a jackass!

He'd sent Manda a query letter, and surprise, surprise...

Attached was a contract from the Roger Peddet Literary Agency!

I opened the Word document and scanned it. "Ghostwriter? *Pink Cupcake Princess* books?" *Maggie's books!*

As annoyed as I was that Dane had gone behind my back and done this, I started to think about it. I could come clean that I was Harry, not Dane the Shakespearean actor. Then she could see I could write more than erotica. Maybe under a pen name…

What am I thinking?

I slammed the laptop shut and paced around the apartment.

I sent her roses yesterday…alluded to a second date. I had to make a decision to live in the present, not beat myself up over the past. Or I'd be hauled off to the looney bin to flirt with the nurses in a gown where my ass would always feel the air conditioning.

What a clever trick, asking me to ghostwrite a little girl's book. I checked my phone. She wanted to see me. I checked her schedule. How apropos. The reclusive "Harry Sackes" was slated to be the guest speaker Wednesday at the EAA conference in Skokie. I usually sent Dane, but I had to tell her the truth. What better way would there be, seeing as "Miss Manda Wolfgram will be taking pitches at the EAA conference tomorrow."

I rubbed my hands together like the evil genius I was. I had a plan.

After tomorrow, either Manda would expose herself as a sell-out money grubbing agent whose delicate sensibilities were a sham or…

Or what?

A part of me wanted her to tell me she hated me. But another part of me wanted her to be the one. The real deal. A woman who deserved the pedestal I already had her affixed to. So badly I wanted answers. Closure. On so many levels.

A text came in with the *Dragnet* theme song. From Dane.

My friends need volunteers for free massages tomorrow night. Meet me at 8 sharp at Eighteen North Wabash. I promise you'll have a chick not a dude. Cool?

A massage did sound good. I needed to relax for what I was about to do. Yes, she'd hate me forever. But I could tell her to join the club. Our second date would be my great reveal at the EAA conference. I had to stay focused. She'd fire me as a client after she heard me speak. I tried to convince myself that the offer to represent me alone was proof positive she was a filthy liar out for money, not the nicey-nice, good girl she played herself out to be.

"Cool," I typed back. Then I printed the document from Manda, signed it, scanned it back in, and emailed it to her.

Surprise!

"Time to announce my news *everywhere*!" I told Desdemona. I let the world know who my hot new agent was via every social media I had at my disposal. I didn't want to upset her apple cart. I had to stick razors in all her apples, coat them with poison, set fire to them, and send the heaping cart careening down the hill into her life.

Time to see exactly who Manda Wolfgram really was.

CHAPTER SEVENTEEN

MANDA

"My thoughts are whirled like a potter's wheel;"
(King Henry the Sixth Part I 1.5.19)

Tuesday Night – 8 sharp

I was supposed to meet Dane at Eighteen North Wabash. He'd slipped a note under my door, and I had to admit I was more than a little excited to see what he had planned. The address didn't ring a bell, but I gave it to the cab driver anyway. The address led me to a refurbished building with a sign in the window, "Sorento's School of Massage." The neon "Open" sign was not lit, and the front door was locked. Cupping my hands, I peeked in the front window and found the place dim.

Did he give me the wrong address? I dug out the note and checked the scribble. Just then, a shadow appeared and unlocked the door, causing me to jump.

A woman dressed in white jeans and a school of massage T-shirt with black hair pulled back in a high ponytail greeted me with a grin. "Are you Manda?"

"Yes."

"Come on in! Don't worry. You're at the right place." She ushered me into a dimly lit private room with the number two hung on the door. Inside were two massage tables. A jet of steam circled upward from an aromatherapy machine emitting a faint scent of spiced vanilla. "You can put your things here." She motioned to a chair. "Take off everything except your underwear. Flip this switch on the wall right before you get on the table, then lie facedown under the blanket. Dane won't come in until you're comfortable." She slipped out the door.

Dane?

Is he a Shakespearian massage therapist?

My heart pounded at the thought of him rubbing my topless form. This was a bit too much, too fast. Maybe he was some kind of freaky weirdo. Maybe this second date thing wasn't such a great idea.

Hopefully, there was still time to flee the scene.

I cracked the door open to find the woman standing right outside. "I'm not entirely comfortable with having Dane massage me. I mean really, we just met." I opened the door wide and grabbed my purse to leave. "But please tell him thanks for the offer."

The girl laughed and pushed me back inside the room. "Oh, it's not like that at all. *I'm* your masseuse. Dane is my friend. My boyfriend and I are new grads from the school, and Dane asked if we'd do a tandem massage for you guys. It's good practice for us. You'll love it. I swear."

I hesitated. After my grueling day at work, which included an actual cake from my boss to congratulate me on—big maybe—signing Harry, a relaxing massage from a trained professional wouldn't be all that bad. I hesitated. "Okay." I stepped back into the room and shut the door. I peeled off my sensible work suit and left on my bra and panties.

That wouldn't do.

Is all this nakedness really necessary? Couldn't the woman rub around my bra?

Oh, what the heck? After heaving a sigh, I unclasped the black lace bra, knowing the massage would be better without it and not really wanting to flaunt my undergarments to a stranger.

I tucked the bra discreetly under my neatly folded blouse and skirt. Then, in one swift movement, I flipped the requisite switch, hopped on the table, and covered myself up to the neck, feeling more exposed than Ned Beatty in *Deliverance*.

I placed my head in the open hole, which gave me a stellar view of the carpeted floor, and waited.

The door opened. "Manda?" Dane's voice was husky. "Well, this is insanely awkward. Stupid, Dane."

"It's fine," I said to the carpet. "Don't be mad at yourself. After the day I had, when I found this note slipped under my door, I was excited at any chance to see you." No chance I'd lift my head; a boob might pop out or something.

Fingertips caressed my scalp, and I melted. "I'm sorry you had a bad day. Do you get a lot of massages?"

"No. To tell you the truth, I've never had one." Sixty-dollar backrubs plus a tip were a luxury I never made a priority. "What a great idea to have a couples massage as a date. She called this a tandem massage or something. I almost bolted, thinking you were the masseur. Isn't that funny?" My stomach did a flip-flop at Dane's idea and the intimacy this forced.

His bare feet padded next to my bed. I didn't dare lift my head to see what level of lack of apparel *he* was comfortable with. Sheets rustled next to me.

Now this is a date!

Soft music from a pan flute surrounded us in pulsing waves reverberating throughout my whole body. The door opened, and the students made their way to the tables. "I'm sorry I didn't introduce myself earlier. I'm Jenny, and this is my boyfriend, Zach."

I exhaled in relief when the girl I'd met earlier touched my shoulder.

"Oil?"

Dane answered for both of us. "Sandalwood for me and peace and calming for Manda, if she likes it."

I was lulled into a haze between the scented oils, the hands working out the knots in my shoulders, the pan flute music, and...Dane.

Something about having him nearby made my body and mind click into place. I had the weirdest feeling ever: I was *supposed* to be here, right now, with him.

The masseuse began on my shoulders. "Peace and calming is a mixture of tangerine, orange, ylang ylang, patchouli, and blue tansy." She held a small open vial under the table by my nose. "Do you like it?"

I murmured my assent and exhaled, letting the woman's fingers work their magic on my tense muscles. From my shoulders and back, she worked her way slowly down my arms to my fingers. Then she worked my legs from the upper thigh to the calf and down to my feet. A moan escaped my lips. *Oops!*

Better, I supposed, than passing gas. I made a mental note to clench if the need arose.

Dane must have heard me make the sound. Willing myself to enjoy the rest of the massage in silence, Dane gave out a yelp, more as if in pain than enjoyment. The guy was probably really cranking on him.

A burst of adrenaline coursed through me. A protective instinct. My heart beat a little faster. My nipples tingled.

Stop the press! My boobs had never done *that* before. It was kind of good weird.

I went with it.

A faint whisper in my subconscious wondered what kind of sounds Dane made when he was...when we would be...

God, I'm such a prude!

I forced myself to say it in my own head: *I wonder if I could make Dane moan with pleasure if we were making love.*

Sex! Call it sex! I chided myself. Vanessa needed to pull a Rizzo from Grease and "Look at me, I'm Sandra Dee" my butt into gear. No one said "making love" anymore.

A scary thought seeped into my head. Was I giving Dane a second chance date, or was he giving me one?

Sexy did not emanate from my pores. More like a nerdy homebody.

Somewhere deep inside, I made a gut decision. I would let my hair down, have Ally sew me into black leather pants, and listen to Dane in the throes of pleasure. Moans *I* caused him to make.

One way or another, I'd make that happen.

As the woman began to work on my other leg, fantasies with Dane consumed me. I now wished it was his expert hands kneading my lower back. How could I ever reciprocate or repay him for this most unique date?

Something else nagged at me.

Harry.

Should I tell him about the Harry Sackes situation? Would he be mad? Probably he'd think I was some kind of fake. Talking Shakespeare and then representing a John Holmes type!

"Please turn over." The female masseuse stood between the tables and held up a blanket so when I flipped over, there would be no issue with modesty. I slid down, and the girl placed a pillow under my knees and neck. Dane was to my left; I flicked my gaze in his direction, but his eyes were closed and he was fully covered. Jenny began to work on my left arm while her boyfriend, Zach, began working on Dane's left arm.

Zach worked rhythmically with frequent glances at Jen. It seemed an aphrodisiac to watch his girlfriend work.

Like my aphrodisiac was watching Dane on stage. I closed my eyes and relaxed.

A bolt of electricity hit me. Something touched my left hand.

Dane.

A lazy, satisfied smile on his face let me know he was enjoying his massage. "You okay?" he said, his voice rough.

I nodded and squeezed his hand between the tables. We lay there hand in hand until the masseurs switched sides.

I tried to let my mind go blank in order to absorb everything: inhale the oils, digest the music, and savor the atmosphere of the best date I'd ever been on. But I was still waiting on that first kiss.

After the massage brought me to a blissful state of utter relaxation, the massage couple and Dane quietly left the room. I basked in the peace for a few minutes before dressing and peeking out the door.

"Did you enjoy that?" Dane sat cross-legged outside the door, eyes turned up expectantly.

A piece of me wanted to crawl into his lap and lavish him with kisses for the experience. "I loved it. Thank you." Then I saw the left side of his face. A long scar ran from his ear down his cheek and ended at his jawbone. I blinked several times, willing myself not to stare. Ah, this was why he'd worn the sideburns. And amazing stage makeup.

He brushed himself off, got up, and took my hand. "I know. I'm ugly. And no, you can't ask about it."

"Stop." I dug my heels in until he stopped. "Let me see."

Turning to face me, he averted his eyes.

"You are not ugly. Don't ever say that." I tried to place my hand on his cheek, but he pulled away. "What do you have in mind now?" The scar meant nothing to me. He was still the most beautiful man I'd ever known. I wanted to kiss away the pain from his scar from top to bottom, but before my runaway train of an imagination got too kinky, he grabbed my hand again and led me out the front door.

His arm jerked out into the road, and he hailed the first cab he could, almost as if he were in a feverish hurry. He opened the door for me, and I slid across to the far end of the seat.

"Where to next?"

He leaned in, lifted my arm, and kissed my hand. "You're going home. Have a nice night. I promise I'll see you soon." He rubbed his hand over his cheek. "And for the record, I was trying to save someone's life. But it didn't work."

I sighed with a half-hearted protest. His mind was already made up. I readjusted to the center of the back seat as a deep disappointment consumed me. Dane prepaid my fare and waved from the sidewalk.

Shoot! All I wanted was to get this gorgeous man alone. And from there, well…I didn't trust myself. Luckily, he was a perfect gentleman. I closed my eyes and let the cab make its twists, turns, and stops on its way back home.

This guy was killing me. Never had I wanted someone this badly.

After dealing with Beefer's bladder, I poured a glass of wine and began to delete query letters, citing my standard line, "Not for me."

No man had ever been "for me." Not until now.

In the middle of two hundred and fifty emails was a note with the subject "SURPRISE! I'M ALL YOURS!" with an attachment containing the signed contract.

From Harry Sackes.

Correction: *agented author* Harry Sackes.

With my stomach in knots, I typed a terse reply:

Dear Mr. Sackes,

You are not MINE. Not yet anyway. Please find the attached unfinished novel you are contractually obligated to finish.

Ms. Wolfgram

CHAPTER EIGHTEEN

HARRY

"Why, then, can one desire too much of a good thing?"
(As You Like It 4.1.118-119)

My whole body shook. In pure rage. I took the stairs two at a time and whipped open the door to our apartment. Dane stood waiting for me with a devilish smile.

My hands curled into fists, and I punched him square in the jaw.

Dane took a step backward but didn't fall. Instead, he cowered and covered his face. "What the heck? I was trying—"

I hit him again, pushed him onto the ground, and went to town. A left. A right. There was blood on my knuckles, and as soon as Dane tried to offer a word, I shut him up with another blow. Then, I rolled off of him, and we both lay on our backs breathing hard.

"Get the fuck out of here. Now."

Dane didn't say a word. He left.

He'd screwed me. I had a plan to end it with Manda. In a

way she would understand and blame me for being greedy. An ending I could have lived with. But Dane had messed it all up.

After two shots of tequila and some ice on my knuckles, I wandered over and stared at my computer screen. I minimized the screen and opened my email.

I read and reread my emails with Manda. I had signed the contract only to let her fire me.

Fuck you, Dane.

There was no good way to fix this.

To offer a reparation. Then I remembered...the contingency.

Finish Maggie's next book. Because Manda never thought I could do it. What did an erotica author know about little girls, princesses, and cupcakes?

My mouse hovered over Maggie's document. I didn't deserve to be happy. To have a girlfriend, live happily ever after. Not after what I'd done. But something tugged at me. A little girl asking me to give it a try. For her. Not for Manda. I'd give it a try for my sister.

Because after Skokie, Manda would never talk to me again. She'd spit in my face, and I deserved it. All the lies.

My inbox was brimming with congratulatory emails about being "agented." My Facebook friends, Twitter followers, and those who read my scathingly hot blog were jacked up about the news of me going mainstream and signing with the Roger Peddet Agency.

Without thinking, I grabbed my tablet and downloaded Maggie's first book for the *Pink Cupcake Princess* series, nestling into my favorite chair to read while eating crackers and guzzling soda. I finished it in record time.

The book wasn't half bad. If you were a ten-year-old girl.

My sister had been eleven.

I pushed the thought away and approached the task with an analytical mind. Double-clicking on the attachment from

Manda, I read to the point where Maggie had typed her last word before the Grim Reaper snatched her. It seemed prudent to google the series, check its sales, and read all her reviews—good and bad.

I made a decision. A parting gift to Manda to ease her pain. But the memories of who I was doing this for rushed and consumed me.

The next thing I knew, I stood in the bedroom looking at a family photo on Dane's dresser. A picture of me, Dane, and…I couldn't allow my memory to form her name. Unconsciously, my mind replayed the day for the umpteenth time.

Ten years prior…

I set up the Slip 'N Slide on the giant hill in our backyard. Freezing cold hose water aside, neighborhood kids had spent the greater part of the morning concocting more and more dangerous scenarios to go down the hill.

We'd already done frontward and backward. On our snowboards. On roller blades.

When my younger sister asked to join in the fun, I said no.

Far too dangerous for a little sister. Much less *my* little sister.

"I don't want you to get hurt. Can't you just watch?"

She sniffed, turned on her heel, and retreated to the garage.

Only to return with a toboggan.

"Uh-oh, Dane," I said. "Evel Knievel is ready to take on the Slip 'N Slide with her luge. Hang on now. Mom will kill me if—"

Before I could stop her, she launched herself down the hill. Halfway down, the sled careened off the plastic, hit the grass, and she tumbled in summersaults down the hill.

I raced to her crumpled form at the bottom of the hill. She

moaned, and I knew there would be hell to pay. Mom wouldn't hesitate murdering me on the street in broad daylight if a hair on my sister's head got hurt.

I knelt next to her and stroked her shoulder. "Are you okay, Sis?"

Writhing around, she grabbed her head. "Ow! I think I hit my head. Who are you?"

I lifted her, and she moaned louder. Her eyes rolled back in her head as I rushed up the hill. The small form of the sister I loved so dearly began to convulse in my arms. Was she having a seizure?

Frozen, I stopped and looked down at her.

She was laughing! "Put me down, silly. I'm fine. It'll take more than that to hurt me. I'm tough, like you!"

Pissed beyond reason, I released her, and she leapt out of my arms, landing on all fours like a house cat. I chased her up the hill and into the house.

Mom came out of the laundry room, wondering about all the brouhaha.

But my sister got the last laugh.

Back outside, the three of us posed for the camera. I propped her up on my shoulders holding an old trophy I had won in a spelling bee. We dubbed her the official gold medal winner of the Slip 'N Slide luge. I remember smiling for the camera.

Click.

Staring at the picture today, I could still hear the click of Mom's Polaroid and see the picture emerge from the bottom of the camera.

Okay. I'd give Maggie's book one evening of my life.

One.

For my sister.

I opened the blackout curtains to let the city lights inside for a few hours. Positioning myself in front of the computer, I began to type. My hands and body shook with each word that appeared on the screen. Every sentence convulsed me with more pain than the last. But I pushed through it, paragraph by paragraph, chapter by chapter, perfecting it and tapping out an ending even my sister would have loved.

But I couldn't hit "send."

Not yet.

CHAPTER NINETEEN

MANDA

"That it should come to this!"
(Hamlet 1.2.137)

Wednesday

I borrowed Dad's car and began the gridlock commute to Skokie for the writers conference after spending much of Tuesday dumbstruck Harry Sackes was now my client and had agreed to the stipulations in my meticulously crafted yet cryptic attachment. I had been left with no choice but to forward Maggie's unfinished manuscript to Harry with an insincere note of "welcome to the family."

He'd butcher the manuscript, and this would be over.

He'd better.

If Harry managed to eke out a publishable ending or if he didn't…well, either way, I was screwed.

He won't, I kept telling myself.

How would I tell Dad—and Pete for that matter—that I now represented erotica? Maybe I could keep it quiet and pass

Harry off to my boss as soon as he ruined Maggie's story. I released my crushing grip on the steering wheel as traffic let up a bit in the burbs. My phone dinged with an incoming text, and I illegally gave it a quick glance.

Dane.

"The secret to humor is surprise…Aristotle."

An odd quote. Was he going to surprise me with something else? Another unfinished date? That would make number three.

I slid into a parking spot at the hotel where the daylong conference was being held. I grabbed my essentials—purse, computer, stack of business cards—and smoothed my gray skirt when I stepped out from the vehicle. My mood was significantly elevated at the thought of another surprise from Dane. Maybe this time, I'd get that first kiss.

Today would go smoothly; I would find the next F. Scott Fitzgerald and be on my way.

Not.

At the check-in table, I found my name badge and asked a volunteer for my list of pitches. A life-size cardboard cutout of Fabio stood nearby, welcoming the aspiring and established authors.

The cutout left a bitter taste in my mouth.

Fake. Unattainable. Womanizer. Better hair than his one true love. His tan, hairless chest puffed out, and his airbrushed face held a look of deep mystery and longing. I stifled a giggle when imagining him tending to his bodily functions like every other regular human.

Women read books, why? To escape their own daily drudges. To escape to an imperfect world where a perfect hero would sweep them off their feet and say, "I am yours alone. I will never love another."

I loved this idealism. Heck, I'd seen it firsthand with my parents. Undying love. The hot passion that ignites the fire between two people though, could that last? Did my father get excited *every* time Mom walked into the room? Did Mom drop everything and run into his arms every time he came home?

Parting is such sweet sorrow...

Dane acted Shakespeare, but did he live it?

"This way, please." The volunteer led me to a well-organized conference reception desk for speakers, agents, and publishers.

"Good morning, Ms. Wolfgram," a woman said, seated on a folding chair. She had short, fuzzy brown hair and no makeup. She wore a knitted sweater, and I noticed the skin of her ankles protruding under the table where her too short black pants ended. "Here is your schedule. I'm sorry it's crammed full, but after the news, I'm sure you can understand why authors have come out of the woodwork and are begging to pitch with you today! Instead of the usual seven minutes per pitch, we changed yours to five so you could accommodate all eighty-four pitches. We'll bring lunch to you so you don't have to stop."

I stuck the name tag to my white blouse and picked up my schedule. "I'm sorry, Edna," I said politely, reading the woman's name tag, "but I couldn't possibly handle eighty-four pitches today. What news are you talking about?"

Edna cupped a hand to her mouth and whispered, "Harry Sackes."

I let my mind utter a long stream of curse words while I backed away and headed for the pitch room. Oh dear. I dropped my leather bag next to the small table set up for me and fled to the bathroom before the onslaught. With my hand on the bathroom door, a finger poked my shoulder.

I turned to see Paul Grooger, a New York agent, who was six inches shorter than I was and sported a full mustache and beard. He had a twinkle in his eyes. "Nice job securing Harry Sackes. He'll make you a mint. I *love* his books."

The twinkle went from the look of a friendly hello to that of a dirty old man whom I realized was eye level with my nipples. "Uh, thanks," I said, rushing to relieve myself before my first pitch. A gaggle of women followed me into the bathroom. I locked the stall and unfastened my skirt when I heard a knock on the stall door.

"Ms. Wolfgram. I wasn't able to get a pitch with you today, but I want you to know I used to write for Half Moon Books before they closed and would love to have the same chance to go to the next level you are giving to Mr. Sackes."

I wiped and pulled up my nylons.

This was ridiculous.

Before I could flush, a business card was slipped under the stall. I picked it up and dropped it into the toilet, watching it swirl and disappear like I wished I could do with this day. "Okay, I'll get back to you."

Four women started talking all at once while I squeezed my way in to wash my hands. They pushed cards in my hand and begged for me to check out their work. They asked if they could mention meeting me at this conference when they queried me. I gave them each a smile and a nod, collected the cards, and rushed from the claustrophobic bathroom to get to my pitch chair.

I wanted to grab a black permanent marker and write on the back of each of their business cards: *Sorry, not for me.*

Usually, attending conferences was a marketing tool for the agency. The chances of finding talent were slim to none, actually. Substance was elusive. Talent was inherited. Skill could be taught, but agents didn't usually possess that kind of time.

Everyone would get my standard nod and a smile and the requisite: "Please send me the first fifty pages and a synopsis, and I'll take a look." This gave the authors hope. Like any good relationship, it was easier to break up over the internet. "It's not you, it's me."

Locked for the day in a room the size of Vanessa's walk-in closet with ice water on a tray as my only sustenance, I had no choice, but to smile, shake hands, sit, and listen.

I exhaled and willed my heart to slow down. Who the hell was this Harry Sackes anyway, and why was he such a big deal? He must have blogged or tweeted about our deal, but how could it have reached this many people already? People seemed enamored with him.

My first pitch, a thirtyish motherly-type, sat down with an awestruck look on her face. Her hands were shaking. "I'm thrilled to meet you. What with your famous new client being the headline speaker this afternoon. I think this is the only conference he's doing all year. Wow, I've never done this before, but I'm so excited for the chance to tell you about my erotic novel called *Space Sex*, where aliens meet with humans in a futuristic orgy told in second person point of view so that…"

I hunkered down and settled in for a long day of pitches and to steel myself for meeting and playing nice with my newest client.

Nearly dragging my starving self to the main hall in the early afternoon, I supposed it was time to meet Harry. He was already on stage giving his speech.

The voice was familiar.

From afar, I watched his hair, his body movements.

Then it hit me.

My new client had arranged the most romantic date I'd ever been on. My new client had cut out after our massage last night. My new client moonlighted as a Shakespearean actor.

My new client was Dane.

The damn lying, sick bastard.

CHAPTER TWENTY

HARRY

*"There's no trust,
No faith, no honesty in men; all perjured,
All forsworn, all naught, all dissemblers."
(Romeo and Juliet 3.2.86-87)*

Back at home, I paced the floor. She up and left. Manda saw me on stage and walked out. No hello. No goodbye. It was done. And I was happy. Wasn't I?

I went back to my computer and reread what I had done for Maggie. My parting gift. I'd made the series better, even editing the stuff that the prim and proper Miss Maggie had already penned before she went belly-up. The book was completely done.

I sent her a final email with the finished book as an attachment:

Manda,

Consider my obligation met and our agreement terminated. You are probably pissed. I wanted money and fame and used you to move me forward on that path. I'll do my best to make sure our paths never cross again.

Dane/Harry

I never wanted to hurt her. But such is life.

My pacing spread to the hallway, arms wrapped tightly around my body. I found myself in the elevator, then the lobby. I circled the leather couch quartet eleven times, muttering to myself, "It's done. Forget it," over and over.

Eleven times round and round in the revolving door before the cool outside air hit me in a rush of summer nighttime ice. I'd forgotten a sweatshirt.

Blinking, I found myself on a barstool at Snickers with an untouched whiskey in front of me. Had minutes passed? Hours? I didn't know. I gave meaningless grunts to people who attempted to engage me in conversation.

More time unaccounted for. The next time I snapped back to reality, two naked girls were posing on my bed, snapping pictures of each other. "Can we be on the cover of your next book?" The girls giggled and began to kiss each other.

"No. Now get out."

Too wrapped up in each other, the girls kept at it, ignoring me all together. They had followed me home.

"See," I said to no one. "Women are sluts, like Dane always said. I had one chance with a good one, and I blew it. My stupid life."

The girls walked out of my bedroom stark naked with their skin glistening in post-coital ecstasy. Their whispers and giggles grated on my ears like fingernails on a chalkboard. They opened a bottle of wine, and finding no glasses, began to chug it directly from the bottle, ignoring me as I swung in circles on the writing chair.

A knock on the door jolted me back to the present. Was the

sun coming up? The girls resumed kissing near our overflowing garbage can, exchanging their wine-laced saliva.

Stooping, I peered through the peephole. Why was *she* here?

Stepping into the hallway, I pulled the door shut behind me.

Manda promptly flung herself into my arms.

My whole body tensed. This was not real. A mirage maybe of what I wanted her to be doing right now. Slowly, I relaxed and allowed my arms to wrap around her waist. Her hair smelled of orchard apples, and I pressed my face into her locks, letting the warmth of her body pass into my frigid form.

I sighed. I actually sighed. For one split second, I thought, *I'm wrong: wrong about my sister, wrong about how I've acted all these years. Manda can forgive me. Forgive everything.* I allowed myself to see a sliver of the pain I'd caused my family by years of good intentions.

"Manda, I can explain." There in the hall, outside my prison, I found a reason to live in her wholesome arms.

She pulled away and gave me a look of...? Admiration? Tenderness? Love? "The story! It's perfect. I never thought you could be so…"

She'd read it.

And inhaled the life I infused inside it. For my sister.

I cradled her face in my hands.

There was something magical in her eyes when she looked at me. Something no one had shown me in years, if ever. She was *proud* of me.

This woman melted me like a blizzard in the Arizona sun. Maybe I could escape. Forego this life and run away. Spend the rest of my life finding ways to impress this woman from here on out.

"I never thought you could be so—" She started again.

The door behind us creaked. "We're bored. Come back in

and join us? We have plenty more ideas for a new book cover," one said.

The other whistled at Manda. "Hey, sweetie, you joining us?"

Manda's face tightened, and she gave me the same look Dane got from women he refused to pay after a fuck. A gaze of utter disgust. "Join you?"

The women behind me were immaterial now, useless whores who had chosen their own paths. Manda *was* the real deal. Capitalizing on the moment, I leaned in to kiss her. With closed eyes, I never saw the hand coming before it made contact with my cheek.

Slap!

Then I was slammed up against the wall in the hallway, getting pummeled. This filly was a bulldozer!

My now-watering eyes registered Manda's brother, Pete, on top of me. Not Manda. The punches hurt, but I didn't care or move to block the onslaught. I deserved them.

A woman screamed. I was vaguely aware of the blinding pain above both my ears and jaw before I blacked out.

CHAPTER TWENTY-ONE

MANDA

"...do you think I am easier to be play'd on than a pipe?"
(Hamlet 3.2.386-87)

Thursday morning

My foot tapped itself against the waiting room floor. Arms crossed, I directed my stare at Harry's assailant—my brother, Pete. They had to keep Harry overnight to make sure he didn't have a concussion and wouldn't let us see him until this morning. This was all my fault. If I'd stayed and talked to him after the convention or not read the finished manuscript and had the stupidity to give him the benefit of the doubt...

Who am I kidding? He writes sex stuff! Of course that's what he'd be doing. Not having tea and crumpets.

Desperate to explain myself, I sat in the waiting room chair next to Pete.

His legs bounced nervously, and he bit his nails on the hand that didn't have a bandage on it from punching.

"Pete, I—"

His phone rang. "Sorry, I have to take this." Answering the call, he stood and paced the floor. The automatic doors leading to the parking lot kept opening and closing every time he passed them, but he didn't seem to notice.

"Hi, Sarah. I miss you, too. I know. Totally my fault. What is Lily doing? Can I talk to her?" He swallowed. Then a look of sheer happiness came over him. "Hi, sweetie. It's Daddy. Uh-huh. She sure is. Auntie Manda says hi. You are? You do?" He put his hand over the receiver. "They are coming to visit!"

I gave him a thumbs-up.

"You want to see the aquarium here, huh? You'll love it. See you soon, boo. Yeah, I'll call later. Bye."

My stomach churned, the heave-ho of nerves, starvation, and utter disappointment. I needed to explain everything to Pete. He deserved it. "Pete, why did you beat him up? You *saw* me slap him."

Pete's eyes were on fire, and his face was drawn. "Look, it's my job to take care of my sister. When I saw you in his arms and his hands all over you, I lost it. He doesn't *get* to be near you after what he did. What was that all about anyway?"

All relaxation from the massage was used up, and my muscles tensed with new worries. *Time to fess up.* "I…my agency, we signed him. Dane or Harry or whoever he's pretending to be. I'm his…agent. I'm so sorry. I was going to tell you and Dad, but we went on two dates and he was like a different person. Kind and sweet. I didn't know until last night that he was playing me." The look of incredulity that passed over Pete's face sank my heart in a lonely pool. Stupid Roger Peddet and his idiotic mandates. Was the job or my puny salary worth it? "My boss found out you met him and forced me into it. But it's only temporary."

Pete seethed but kept his temper under control. "Go on."

"Maggie's husband called me. You know, my best-selling

children's author that suddenly died. He's broke. I was desperate for someone to ghost write the second *Pink Cupcake Princess* book. I told Roger I'd only sign Harry if he agreed to ghost write the rest of the book. I promise I never thought he'd say yes. But, he did."

His face softened when I grasped his hands. His shoulders slumped, and his tense body relaxed into understanding.

"He finished the book. I'm not sure when…or how. But he did it. And even with all the smut, what he wrote for Maggie was nothing short of literary magnificence. I went up to thank him, thinking the alter ego of Harry Sackes was all an act and he *is* the great guy I first met. Obviously, I was wrong." I gulped back the lump in my throat, thinking about the end of Maggie's book. Genius. Compassionate. Eloquent.

Who was Harry Sackes? If he was so skuzzy, how did he pen magic in a little girl's book? Streak-free editing. A polished manuscript. Ready for the publisher. Pete had been right from the beginning. With the right agent, Harry could use his skills for the powers of good, not a reader's erotic one-night stand.

"He did that for you?"

I nodded. I had fallen for a man with a split personality. Just my luck.

A nurse in teal scrubs and a shaggy haircut tapped my shoulder. "You can see him now."

I stood on my tiptoes and gave Pete a kiss on the cheek. "Give me five minutes to talk to him. Figure this out once and for all. Then we can go."

"I'm sorry I overreacted."

The nurse clopped away. After giving my brother a quick wave, I scurried after her.

I hated being anywhere near a hospital. After my mother's death, I vowed never to step foot in a hospital again. But there was no way I would have left without giving Harry a piece of my mind.

He had a cool white washcloth over his eyes and was holding an icepack to his head.

"Hey, I hear you're going to live."

"See, you do care."

"Oh, I care all right." I made my way to the end of the hospital bed, a weird déjà vu filling me with all the old memories of being in a room exactly like this, visiting Mom. "I care that you are nothing like you said. I care that you lied to me. I care very much that you kept your word and finished Maggie's book in record time. Now, let me tell you what I don't care about. I don't care about liars. About games. Or about being your agent or your girlfriend. Don't call me. Don't text me. Don't try to see me. Write whatever you want, and stay the hell out of my life."

I turned to leave as he protested.

"Manda, wait! It's not like that!"

But I didn't wait to hear the next lie. It didn't matter. Tears streamed down my cheeks, and I brushed them away. Were they sadness or anger? Probably a little bit of both.

Pete hailed us a cab while I punched in Roger Peddet's digits. *This* was worth waking up the old fart.

"Holy shit, Manda, it's late. What is it?"

"The book's done. *Harry Sackes*—your new client—finished it, and it sparkles like the morning sun on the ocean. It's exceptional and ready for the editor."

"You can't be serious."

"Yes, sir."

"Great, send it to George at the publisher. I'll tell State Street bookstore we are still a go for Monday now that I know we will have a next book in the series. We have to keep up the momentum. You will be the 'princess' on Monday, and find out more about that cupcake recipe. Maybe it is worth something. I'll call my friend at the paper and get an article run on Sunday about the event, seeing as kids are off from school next week.

No problem for you, right? A 'real' princess and cupcake party for Maggie's best seller?"

Impossible. "As long as you agree to take on Mr. Sackes. I'm done with him. Forever."

"Deal. Make this event a smash and you'll not only be able to pawn off Harry Sackes to me, I'll consider you a senior agent. Stay in touch."

It was Thursday. Four days. If I could pull this off, Harry would no longer be my client, and that was worth everything to get my life back to normal.

Time to mobilize the troops.

Pete snoozed next to me in the back seat of the cab.

Opening my purse, I dug out my phone, hoping for a miracle. "Vanessa? Hey, it's me. I'm leaving the hospital and need your help."

"The hospital?" she screeched. "What happened?"

"I'm fine. Pete beat up Romeo. It's a long story. I'll tell you all about it. Hey, what's the best bakery in Chicago?"

"I know several. Why? Are you hungry?" She yawned, her voice still heavy with sleep.

I laughed. "No, silly. Can you meet me at Allison's first thing tomorrow morning? I need help, the kind only my two best friends can provide."

"Sure, anything you need. Why at Ally's?"

"'Cause we need her mammoth mommy kitchen. We're making cupcakes."

CHAPTER TWENTY-TWO

HARRY

"The miserable have no other medicine
But only hope:"
(Measure for Measure 3.1.2-3)

Dane slid back the curtain to my bed and grimaced. "You look like shit, Bro."

"Thanks," I said, examining my puffy face. I had a nasty cut on my lip, and tomorrow my face would look like it had been dipped in melted crayons. "Worse than normal?"

Dane gave me a shit-eating grin. "Nah, we're twins. Now we match." He leaned up against the wall, eating applesauce clearly meant for me. He wore his favorite Sox baseball hat, sunglasses to hide the black eye I'd given him, and a pink Death Metal T-shirt with a rainbow.

"Can I borrow those sunglasses when we leave?"

"Yes. Isn't this about done? Just tell Manda the truth. She'll understand."

I hopped out of bed and grabbed my T-shirt and jeans. "You think? It was me up there with those girls. It's me who writes the smut. It's me who lied to her from day one. Nope. It's over. See, that's what happens when I start to care." I wanted Dane to yell at me. Blame me. Tell me I was the bad guy.

But he wouldn't. He shrugged and threw the empty applesauce container into the trash. He'd never once blamed me for anything. And I hated that about him. "So what's next?"

"Stick to the plan." *My plan.* A plan of sick revenge. A plan that hadn't gotten us any closer to our sister's killer than the day I'd hatched the crazy plot. "Vito's supposed to call me today."

Dane fiddled with the crisp white hospital sheets to avoid looking at me.

"What?" I asked.

"I'm out. We're dropping the plan. I refuse to do this anymore. I have a chance to become a company actor at an outdoor Shakespeare theater in Wisconsin, and I want to do it."

What could I say? He was right. "Give me a little longer. If this tip is a dud, we can bail. Get a fresh start. But let me have one more chance to finish what we started. We made a deal, shook on it."

"Fine," he conceded. "Even though one hot tamale woman with glasses was almost enough for you to throw in the towel. Ditch everything we worked for. You didn't seem to mind." He paused. "And neither did I. That's why I set you up on that date. I'm hoping you can move on someday, be happy."

I hated that he was right. But who was I to even entertain the idea of me with a girl like her? I didn't deserve her.

Before we left the hospital, I got a call from Vito saying to meet him at the jellyfish exhibit at the aquarium in two hours with cash. Dane lent me his baseball hat and sunglasses before I left the condo.

"Good luck," he said.

I slid into a cab with my coat stuffed full of envelopes of cash and got dropped off on the thoroughfare connecting the planetarium, the aquarium, and the massive museum, deciding it was better to be early than run late. An attendant waved me around to the front of the building, past a gigantic water fountain shaped like a man hugging a fish the same size as me, which spewed water into the penny-filled fountain. The main entrance resembled the Lincoln Memorial with a staircase that seemed like it could have been the setting of the *School House Rock* video "I'm Only a Bill." Up the stairs through a covered walkway, patrons were shunted through the revolving doors and into the main entrance where I paid a bored-looking girl my entrance fee.

In front of me, a little girl tugged at her dad's arm with the urgency only a child can demand. "Can we go into the Amazon Rising exhibit first?" the little girl asked, clapping her hands.

"Sounds good to me."

I knew that voice: Manda's brother, Pete. The threesome in front of me must have been Pete, his estranged wife, and daughter. It was hard to miss the resemblance between the little girl and her aunt. I followed them, keeping my distance. I found out the little girl's name was Lily. She was eager to point out her favorite animals from the Amazon: the yellow-spotted Amazon river turtle munching leaf lettuce and the black-legged poison dart frog whose body was an earthy orange.

I eavesdropped on Pete and Sarah while Lily was enraptured in the Waters of the World exhibit with the giant Japanese spider crab.

"…can't come back…"

"…please don't be mad…dumb thing to do…"

The duo sounded destined for marital disaster.

They never once looked around or noticed me. I followed

cackling families and hands-on fathers excited for a day with their families. It made me feel hollow inside.

That would never be me. I couldn't have Manda.

No due justice.

Lily marched on. California sea lions. Snow white beluga whales opening and closing their blowholes when they surfaced. Sea otters floating on their backs, using their paws to eat, and playing with each other, flipping over and over in the water. Must be nice. No stress. Not a care in the world. Someone tossed them morsels on a regular basis. No predators in sight.

Free.

I stood in the mayhem that was my life while a fuzzy-looking otter danced through the water without a care in the world.

I released a puff of air that threatened to suffocate me like I was being held underwater by one of these sea creatures. I still had time, so I kept pace with Lily and her parents, who stopped to watch the dolphins being fed their afternoon fish, then worked their way through the starfish and sea urchin touch tank.

Entering the jellyfish exhibit behind them and still ten minutes before I was supposed to be there, I entered a new surreal environment. New age music was piped into the exhibit, and the kaleidoscope of colors behind the different variations of jellyfish turned my brain psychedelic. Moon jellies. Blue jellies. The lion's mane jellies with their long stringy appendages moving in rhythmic time to music they could not hear.

And then Vito appeared. He handed me a manila folder. I slipped him an envelope while pretending to look at the lion's mane jellies. When I looked again, Vito was gone.

Lily was in the corner doing pirouettes next to the ballerina jellyfish.

I was doing this so little girls like her would stay safe.

CHAPTER TWENTY-THREE

MANDA

"Chewing the food of sweet and bitter fancy"
(As You Like It 4.3.102)

After telling the agency I wouldn't be in until after lunch, I cabbed to the store to collect the cupcake recipe ingredients and headed over to Allison's.

Cute, matching, attached townhouses lined the quiet road. Black metal gates protected each resident's meager yard space, which fit one mommy lawn chair and one kid's push toy.

The tiny push lawn mower was tipped on its side, so I scooped it up and tapped on the front door. Allison greeted me with a huge grin, sporting a messy ponytail and wearing her mom-friendly long pajamas and fuzzy slippers. She pushed up her glasses with the hand not holding her coffee cup. "Damn, was I ever as young as you?"

"Let me in, you dork. We're the same age. One of these weekends, you'll have to get a sitter, doll up, and we'll go out for drinks. We big girls need play dates too, you know." I winked. Ally always told me she thought it must be exciting to have a cool job as a literary agent downtown, while I fantasized about putting on tutus and watching Disney movies all day.

"Sounds good to me," she whispered, pointing to her eighteen-month-old, who snoozed in his Pack 'n Play. "You came during morning nap. The baby will be down until about eleven, and Elias is a wild card. No telling how long we've got." After setting down her coffee, she struggled a bit to pick him up. He sighed contentedly and wrapped his arms around her with a huge sigh, snuggling a sweaty, cute little head onto Ally's shoulder.

I gave him a quick peck on the cheek and mouthed, "So cute!" before they disappeared down the hall and upstairs.

After setting down the grocery bags on the speckled kitchen island, I plucked off my sensible heels and hung up my coat by the front door.

Last night's pomegranate martini mix sat on the counter next to two used glasses. At least they had fun alcohol in her house. Gotta love that.

When she got back, I caught her up on the details of the sixth-floor hottie turned Wolverine Romeo and his alter ego Harry Sackes. "Tricked by an erotica author who moonlights as a Shakespearean actor. Who'd have thought?"

She poured a cup of coffee. "So he lured you in with the actor thing, then you signed him as Harry, and he finished Maggie's book? But I really kind of liked him when I met him. I tell you…the whole world's going nuts!"

Unpacking the grocery bag, I handed her the recipe. "And to top it off, I have to dress up like a princess, hope this cupcake recipe rocks, and pull off a book party on Monday. Ugh!" I threw my hands up in the air.

Ally switched on the radio, not too loud to wake the kids, but enough for us to jam while we baked. "So let's see what's so special about this recipe." Her eyes skimmed the paper, and she shrugged. "A couple of unique ingredients, I guess. I don't know yet. Let's get baking. We'll make it against a standard recipe and taste test." Navigating her kitchen with the quick skills of a master baker, she pulled out measuring cups, bowls, a mixer, and cake decorating supplies. "So, are you sure you aren't going to give Darry a second chance? Do you like that? Dane and Harry are Darry. Or I could call them Hane, but I don't like that as much."

Before I could respond, the doorbell chimed. Vanessa didn't wait, slamming through the front door and sashaying into the kitchen. "You know what goes well with cupcakes? Mimosas!" Producing two bottles of champagne and a half gallon of orange juice, she plopped them in front of us, right between the flour and baking powder.

"Thank goodness!" Ally sighed. "I'm out of Bailey's for our coffee, and I did *not* know how I would ever entertain the two of you." Teetered high on a kitchen barstool, Ally retrieved three champagne flutes from a backlit top shelf of a kitchen cabinet.

"I have to go to work after lunch," I piped up. "So only OJ for me."

"Nonsense," Vanessa said, popping the champagne with a bang and letting the fizz run into the kitchen sink. "You have orders to make a huge bookstore party happen on Monday. We'll simply be busy here all day!"

I did have a lot to do. We needed to test this recipe, figure out what was so special about it, and then find a bakery to make hundreds of them. I needed to go to the bookstore and organize the signing. *Oh crap!* Where was I going to get a princess dress?

I sipped the mimosa placed in front of me. Fine, just one. It was bound to be a long day.

Ally made quick work of doubling both cupcake recipes.

"Can I help?" I wanted to do something more than sit there and watch.

Ally gave a knowing nod to Vanessa as if they were in a sorority that was about to haze and then reject me. "On one condition. Hand me the next ingredient on the list and start again on the story of the fall of the sixth-floor hottie, and don't leave anything out!"

Sighing, I sipped my citrus adult beverage. Maybe I did need a day off. I recounted the whole sordid week. Vanessa's mouth gaped all the way onto the kitchen counter. Lifting the mimosa, she downed it in one gulp and poured another. She tied an apron over the maxi dress that probably cost as much as Ally's fancy mixer. Funny to see someone who touted herself as so fancy content getting flour on her hands and licking frosting from her fingers.

Vanessa had to interject. "I saw...his balls. He was dangling them in a girl's face to demonstrate the Cincinnati Bowtie for a book!"

"I still don't get it," I admitted.

They both laughed. "Because from the woman's perspective, it looks like a bowtie," Ally explained. "Someone hand me the baking soda."

"Ooooohhhhhhhh." I got it now. "Eeeeeeeewwwww!"

Ally huddled us all together. "Group hug!" We formed a triangle of tangled arms. "That is one crazy story. Usually Vanessa has the good stories, but you win on this one, Manda!"

"Let's have a toast." Vanessa lifted her glass. "To men, who are always after one of two things: sex or money!"

Ally was the first to clink Vanessa's glass. I left mine sitting in front of me. "So this is the world I live in?"

"I was at the bank the other day, and this old man walked in and sat down with a banker. He was talking loudly, so I could hear everything," Ally started. "He said he needed to wire money to his son in another state because he had furniture being delivered and had no money. I looked at the bank teller and shook my head. I said to her, 'How long have you been doing this job?' She told me over thirty years. I asked her if she thought money was the root of all evil. Do you know what she said?"

We shook our heads and waited.

"She said, 'Yes, after all I've seen as a banker, I'd say those with no money will do anything to get it and those who already have money will do anything to get more.'"

I clamped my mouth shut. Vanessa and Ally were not hurting. They'd never had to scrounge change to buy a soda or live off noodles until payday. They didn't understand. But I loved them anyway. I would not do anything for money. And this was the last time I compromised who I was for some stupid job.

Putting a sisterly arm around me, Vanessa consoled me. "What a sicko! Stay away from him. Far away. He's a wack job." She hiked up her skirt and hoisted herself up on a chair. "O Romeo, Romeo! Wherefore art thou *real* Romeo?" she began.

She had us in stitches with her terrible acting and overly dramatic Juliet. Ally was even snorting mimosa out of her nose by the end of the botched monologue.

Three mimosas later, we had two pans in the oven and settled in to wait for the cupcake miracle that was about to transpire. I cocked a thumb at the sewing machine strewn with fabric in the corner. "Making the kids clothes now, too, Betty Homemaker?"

"No, I'm making my own role-playing outfits. They are so expensive online. I can make them better myself. Did I tell you about my trip to the ER?"

Vanessa and I shook our heads.

"Are you okay?" Vanessa asked.

"What happened?" I asked.

"Well, against your better judgment, I *did* read *Fifty Shades of Grey*. I thought a little consensual S&M would be fun, so I bought a ball gag and some handcuffs. Sadly, I ordered the wrong size and managed to dislocate my jaw with the ball gag."

"You *what?*" Neither of us could contain our laughter on that one.

"Oh yeah, imagine this. I have a bathrobe over a leather bra and panties. Mark, with the kids in tow, wheels me crying into the emergency room where they ask me to disrobe and question what happened. My jaw hurts so bad I can't talk and am crying, so of course, the kids are crying, and I think Mark and the doctor were crying tears of mirth at my distress. Then *pop*! The doctor snaps my jaw back into place."

It was rare that Vanessa was speechless.

"I told you not to read that book! Your poor mandible!" I chastised before falling into more fits of laughter.

"So needless to say, we canned the feeble S&M attempt to save on our medical deductible, and I'm back to naughty Catholic schoolgirl outfits where he reprimands me with *plastic* rulers only," Ally said, telling the story like she'd sprained an ankle and the doctor had advised switching from jogging to taking long walks. Holding up a red plaid miniskirt and a barely there white cotton shirt, she asked, "Very Brittany Spears, don't you think?" When she replaced her half-sewn garments, she pressed them straight with her hands like she was handling her grandmother's antique wedding dress. "The ER doctor told us that the only case stranger than mine was when some senior citizens came in because he lost his cock ring *up there* in his old lady." She whispered the words "up there" like she was swearing in church. "She complained she needed more lube at her age and that's why it got stuck!"

"That'll be me someday." Vanessa took deep breaths and rubbed her belly. "I'm telling you, a laugh fest like this lets me get out of Pilates class today for sure. Did I ever tell you about that guy that asked me to get a chocolate enema and—?"

Beep. Beep. Beep.

Saved by the oven timer. "Please, for the love of God and all that is holy, hold your tongue, woman!" I covered my ears. "I want to try to enjoy these cupcakes."

The monitors registered that the baby was awake, so we hurried to frost three cupcakes. Vanessa packed some up so as to take samples with her to a few bakeries and check prices. I planned on leaving from here to head over to the bookstore and work out the details of my authorless book signing.

"Quick, let's have a bite before I go get the baby." Ally opened her mouth and took a big bite.

Vanessa unwrapped the small delight, and I dug into the one with the most frosting.

We chewed.

Uh-oh.

Ally spit hers out into the sink, and Vanessa released the contents of her mouth into the nearest garbage can.

I knew the worth of the recipe and forced down the most horrible-tasting thing ever with a large gulp.

The cupcake recipe Maggie Monroe had paid dearly for was…worthless.

CHAPTER TWENTY-FOUR

HARRY

"Time, thou anticipatest my dread exploits"
(Macbeth 4.1.144)

Flipping open the manila envelope, I almost puked. Girls' pictures. Young girls. Each marked only with a number. They looked real bad. But their lives were about to go from bad to worse. And I could only save one. How the hell could I choose? I wanted to save them all.

Placing all the pictures facedown on the floor, I switched them around like a magician. I closed my eyes and picked a card. Grabbing my phone, I sent Vito a text:

Number three.

Minutes later, I got a return message:

Monday 11:30 sharp. You have 120 minutes.
Downtown tower with T. Only for you!

And that's how easy it was in the underworld to get two hours to myself with a child. As I'd told Manda, money talks. Maybe with a gun to Vito's head, he'd tell me where the others were.

Another call and a meeting in a dark alley, where transactions of this sort went down smoothly. The piles of bills should be enough. The guy's selection was slim, but when time was of the essence, one needed to make concessions.

"That one," I pointed.

"Of course." The man licked his finger and began methodically counting the bills. After a satisfied nod, he handed me a paper bag, and I double-checked the contents.

"You know how to use that?" He reached forward, and I jerked back.

Trust issues never die. "Yeah, I know how. Now bounce, man. There's more than enough money in there to forget my face. Understood?"

Stained teeth smiled back at me. "Nice doing business with you." The man was already closing his car door.

I hated to rely on scum for this, but there was no other way. Back in the condo, I punched in the code to our lockbox and hid my purchase.

I needed company so I didn't lose my mind. With Dane doing actor stuff, I decided to blow off some steam in the comfort of my own home, waiting for the final showcase showdown.

I picked up my house phone and found the contact I wanted.

"Hello, Harry." Her voice was soft and buttery. I took a deep, cleansing breath and settled into an open spot on the couch.

"Can you come over?"

"Sure, but with this kind of short notice, it'll cost extra."

I patted the wad of cash in my pocket. What the hell? Might as well go out with a bang.

Two hours and a fierce Scrabble game later, I made Susan promise to get off the streets. I gave her every dollar I could find, somewhere well over $30K. She gave me a kiss on the cheek, gathered her things, and left. I prayed I'd never see her again.

But the street was a siren call when the city's atmosphere changed from sunlight to city light. There was never true darkness in a city. It was always lit up and eager to say, "Come out and play." I opened the blinds of the apartment and watched the people scuttle by on the pavement. I looked up, longing for something I hadn't seen in years—stars.

An odd thing to wish to see. On clear nights, I could see stars here, of course. But not like in the wilderness. I longed to see the smoky path of the Milky Way snaking through the night sky. I wanted the irritation of mosquitoes at dusk and the joy of catching a firefly.

Maybe—if I lived—I would take a trip. A writing sabbatical, so to speak. The four walls of the apartment suddenly felt suffocating. Opening the sliding door, I stepped out onto the balcony. The stank of the city burned my nostrils, so I swirled my vodka lemonade in standard Dean Martin fashion and threw back the contents of the glass.

It, too, tasted foul.

I had gone wrong in this life, and it was too late to change.

Back at the laptop, I killed all the lights inside the apartment again and pulled the shade darkeners over the windows. Darkness was my most faithful mistress. Punctual. A true performer of the same beautiful feats time and again. A traitorous bitch when she insisted on leaving me every morning.

Rocking back in my computer chair, I clasped my hands behind my head and waited for sunrise and the start of my last Sunday in this hellhole existence.

Tomorrow would change everything.

I could feel it.

The phone rang right at our rescheduled time, seeing as I would be indisposed on Monday. "Yeah, yeah," I started. "Let's get this show on the road, Doc. I'm a busy man."

"Good morning to you, too, Harry. How were the last few days?"

"It's been a week, I tell ya. I finished that kiddie book for my new agent, who said it was fab. But, of course it is. I mean, I'm a talented son of a bitch. I dunno, life is pretty fucking good. And speaking of fucking, I'm pretty sure I'll be hooking up with my agent soon."

"Interesting."

Did this idiot doctor *ever* listen to me? At this point, was I an afterthought? A lost cause? Because I had made some real progress this week, and if I couldn't share the moment with my therapist, then who *could* I share it with? Oh yeah, ninety-nine percent of the crap I spouted was bs.

Time to have some fun. "So, I'm thinking about giving up porn, pulling out my great American novel, and heading to a remote cabin to write."

"Good, good. Tell me more." A slurping sound and the rustling of a newspaper told me I still didn't have the therapist's rapt attention.

"But before I bail, I'm going to come and find you and your family, hold you hostage, then murder you all for not helping me get better."

"You know threatening me is grounds for termination of our contract, and I can recommend that you be placed involuntarily in an institution. Would you like to rephrase that last comment, Mr. Sackes?"

So he *was* listening! He just didn't give a rat's ass about me. "I retract the last comment and am going to ask for a new therapist. You suck ass. And coming from me, that really is a derogatory statement. You like the easy paycheck from phoning in. You stopped listening to me or trying to help me a year ago. One single, decent woman has done more for me in one week than you've ever done."

"Renegotiating our contract is done on a bi-annual basis. If you terminate early, that would be a breach of contract, and who would prescribe all your medications?"

I laughed. "I haven't popped a pill from my mail order pharmacy in over two years. I'm off the crazy juice, and I'm about to jump off the train. Refer me to a *female* PTSD-specialized therapist, or your wife will get an earful from me about the sick questions you ask on my forum...*Lance*."

Silence hung in the air between us. I had him. If the good doctor thought I was an imbecile who couldn't put together his fake name on the naughty forums with who he really was, he really didn't know that my hard-earned money bought me any information I wanted.

"Doctor Cynthia Silver is a wonderful psychiatrist. Consider our relationship benignly severed. Expect a call from her next week."

"Fuck you, too. Have a great life being a money-grubbing, good-for-nothing shrink. Never forget I have enough dirt on you to send your wife and career into a tailspin. Capisce?"

Then I thought of something.

"One more thing, you will put in paperwork that I'm cured, have no need for mandated sessions, and they will be done at my leisure with my choice of doctor."

"It's been a pleasure working with you, Harry. All the best."

"Fuck off."

We hung up.

CHAPTER TWENTY-FIVE

MANDA

"Of all base passions, fear is the most accursed"
(King Henry the Sixth Part I 5.2.18)

"No, Roger, that won't be a problem." *Yes, it would.* "Of course, I can handle that." *No, I can't.* "I do realize my job is riding on this. You never stop telling me about all the hungry interns who want my job." *That part is true.*

My blood pressure rose. My hands were shaking, and my heart was pounding. I was making promises I may or may not be able to deliver on. Professional cupcakes. A prince and a princess.

I was in over my head. No mouth-watering cupcake recipe. No prizes, giveaways, balloons… What about glitter?

"I got it. It *will* go off without a hitch."

My next call was to our receptionist. At home. I begged her and promised her a signed copy of all of Harry's books if she would order prizes, balloons, and a few hundred pink cupcakes from any bakery in the city at any price.

Crossing my fingers, I tackled my next task.

Now I was in a full-on panic. Concentration eluded me with the mountain of tasks on my to-do list. And where had my weekend gone? I'd barely slept a wink. I needed to head over to the bookstore as soon as it opened and plan out the logistics of where the signing would be and how to handle door prizes and snacks.

Kill me now. This is never going to work, and I'm going to be looking for a new job next week.

A knock sounded at my door, and a peephole check confirmed it was Pete and Lily. What were they doing up this early on a Sunday morning? I flung the door open, and Lily flew into my arms.

"Auntie Manda! I saw the jellyfish!"

"Hi, Lily. You are so beautiful, like a little princess." I turned to Pete. "I need help today if you can. I'm headed over to the bookstore as soon as they open this morning and…" I rattled off my lengthy task list.

"Watermelon," he said.

I paused in my ramblings. "What watermelon?"

Pete sometimes exuded a calm Zen-like patience that did not exist in my piece of genetic makeup. He got it from Mom. "If I say 'watermelon' to you, it means calm down and take a step back."

"Like a trigger word?" I wanted to calm down but wasn't sure anything would work at this point. Frantic anxiety was on the verge of consuming me.

"Manda, take a deep breath, and tell me what else you can do right now."

∼

Once Pete, Lily, and I stepped into the bookstore, I was able to take that deep breath. Opening my e-reader never compared to the smell of new books. Crisp pages, hard covers, the smell of pine still lingering on the newly typeset pages that were being seen for the first time.

A love-hate relationship with books. That was what I had. Reading would always be my passion, but e-readers were so much nicer to the environment. Everywhere my vision went...books.

Ornate covers. Plain covers. Hard covers. Soft covers. Magazines. Graphic comics. To me, reading was the only good way of escaping reality, or visiting places I might never see, or touching on realms of possibilities I never thought existed.

Knowledge was understanding. And understanding was life. I squeezed Lily's hand. "I seriously don't get in here enough. The library smells like old books, but this place smells like unabashed freedom."

"I like it here, too, Auntie Manda."

Pete led us into the tiny coffee shop within the store. The idea of a quiet cup of coffee sounded soothing before hammering out the details with this usually hostile staff. I had first asked to deal with Brent but had been told he was no longer working here. Likely, they'd stick me with some stuffy historical fiction buff who'd never organized a children's book party before.

But that stress could wait. Pete ordered two mocha lattes and even treated Lily to a chocolate chip scone.

We slid into a quiet table behind a stark sign that indicated no beverages were permitted in the store.

"Thanks, Pete."

I raised an eyebrow. "How are things going with the visit?" I tried to speak in code, but he knew what I meant. *How are you and Sarah?*

"Moving along, which road though is still hard to say. She wants perfection, and I'm not sure I can offer that."

My fingers found warmth around the beverage. "Sorry." I was no one's perfect girl. I was frumpy, wore glasses, practically fell over in high heels, and read other people's words and found the arrogance to pass judgment on them as a career. "I'm far from perfect."

"Cheers to that, Sis." Pete held up his cup in a mock toast, and we sipped our caffeine.

"Can I ask you a question?"

He nodded, licking the whipped cream off of his upper lip and making "mmm" sounds.

"What do you think made her fall for you in the very beginning?"

"I thought it was my winning looks and great personality." He acted offended.

He was goofing around because Lily was with us, so I decided to drop it. Maybe I could help by talking to Sarah later…alone. My thoughts returned to Harry. His words replayed in my head, mingling with my insecurities and realizations about his true intentions the whole time: win me over with Shakespeare and then dupe me into being his agent.

So why finish Maggie's book? It didn't make sense.

I took in the other customers of the coffee shop. Two teenagers on their phones, coffees in front of them, but neither one talking or interacting with each other. An older man with a ripped T-shirt paging through a sale rack paperback. And a middle-aged woman in the corner on an e-reader. Was she lost in the throes of a romance novel with a hot man seducing his one and only? Did the heroine finally meet her Mr. Right? But alas, it was not meant to be…

Maybe I should pick up my coffee and go commiserate with my future self at the e-reader table.

"Manda." Pete was snapping his fingers in my face. "What's wrong?"

"Nothing, it's fine. I still don't get this whole Harry thing. Something about it doesn't make sense."

Pete rolled his eyes. "You are the smartest dumb person I've ever met. Can't you tell if a guy likes you?"

"I assume you are karma, coming around to bite me in the ass. You're about to utter those three fateful words to me that I've said to so many. Go ahead, I'm ready. 'He's…not for you, Manda.'"

"I wouldn't be so fast to judge. Did you ever give him a chance to explain? After the conference? After he finished the book? No. You jumped to your own fast conclusions, and that's not fair. I know I reacted and beat up the guy, but now I'm being judged wrongly, and it sucks not to have anyone ask me my side of the story. I'm not saying marry the guy. Just let him have a chance to explain. Maybe he wants to kick his past to the curb and dive into the relationship pool? If you'll have him."

If I'll have him?

Dumbstruck. Speechless. The world was happening around me, but I froze. In one second, everything was on the table and the crossroad of my life was in front of me. A man who maybe had no other way to tell me something, wrote it to me instead. And I missed it.

And the one thing I couldn't imagine would happen…did.

I got scared. All the memories flooded back to me at once. The email from Harry. The stories from Pete and Vanessa. The suave author addressing the writers at the conference. Him having girls in his room and trying to invite me in for a threesome.

None of it made sense!

"Watermelon." Pete reminded me. "Never thought about it that way, huh?

After tossing their empty cups, Pete and Lily trailed behind me to meet the bookstore's management team. It consisted of Pat, a petite woman with a stark, black bun wearing a printed skirt and white blouse, and Kenny, a lanky, white-haired man who wore a short-sleeve navy button-down shirt that was unbuttoned so far as to expose his heavy smattering of gray chest hairs.

These are the people helping set up a children's book party?

After an elevator ride to the second floor, the employees worked their way to a corner area stocked full of wooden train play sets, puzzles, and stuffed animals. They pointed to a cluttered area near the checkout counter.

"Then the parents can pay for the book and still see their child," the man explained.

A whole new side of me erupted on the spot. Demanding, bossy, and authoritative.

"We will not be stuck up here. We need to be front and center in the store. This book is a New York Times best seller! Move a makeshift register to the front. I want to see lines extending out the front door. Balloons, cupcakes, and each little girl will have her book signed by a professional princess representing the Cupcake Princess from the series. Also, a prince will be on hand to give each little girl a tiara." I elbowed Pete and whispered, "You're up for it, right?"

That's when it got ugly. Me versus the bun lady.

"Well, I should say!" Bun Lady screeched, her bun wiggling around on her head. "That is not our protocol, and I will not be bossed around in my own store. The author is dead, and you want hired actors to hand out cupcakes?" She gesticulated and interrupted me anytime I tried to speak.

Things were getting hairy.

"My author lives on…with her words! She deserves this extra exposure."

The calm man kept trying to interject but ended up stretching out his arms to separate the two of us, who were now pointing at each other.

Another employee showed up while Pete and Lily seemed to be enjoying the show. A young girl with mousy brown hair and glasses tapped the bun lady on the shoulder. "There's a call for you on one."

"Not now," she snapped at her underling.

"But...it's Gary."

The bun lady's head snapped around, and she stomped off after mousy. "Watch them, Kenny, and don't agree to anything," she hissed over her shoulder.

"Seems like a nice lady who loves kids." Pete addressed his comment to the male employee, who couldn't help but smile. "What's the big deal with having this on the main level anyway? And who's so important she left to take his phone call?"

"The big boss." He cowered slightly from my trembling anger. "I understand you want to be downstairs, but we aren't allowed to do that even for big names. Pat is a stickler for rules and is constantly worried about theft and crowd control, no matter about the security tags in the books and at the doors. All she cares about is shrink from theft. I think she figures, if we send everyone up here, we can have more control and make sure no one walks out without paying."

"Don't be a peacekeeper, Kenny. Peacekeepers don't necessarily keep the peace." I tried to allow my words to come out soft and pleasant. "I need ideas and action. What about if we paid for added security?"

Kenny hovered near Pete. "New cameras were recently installed all over the store, so that might be something to remind her about. I guess we did have one big shot sign front and center before." He scratched his chin. "Who was that guy again? Writes fiction or something."

Pete shot me a grin, and I softened my posture a little. Kenny was only trying to help.

Bun-wearing Pat marched back over to our group, and I could almost hear the Wicked Witch music playing in her head. Da-dada Da Dun-dun. "Gary, the owner, asked me to acquiesce to all of your *demands*...I mean, wishes," she said with a fake smile. "So, let's go over everything again, this time downstairs." Her voice held the disdain born from necessitated obedience.

Once we left the store, I clapped my hands. Success!

"You did amazing in there," Pete said.

"I did?"

His brotherly encouragement was like butter on dry popcorn. Pass the salt.

"I was crazy mean, wasn't I? I'm sorry, but poor Maggie..." The words hung on my lips. "Not even here to enjoy her success." My vision got hazy as tears filled my eyes.

"I'm proud of you. You stood up for what you believed in and never backed down."

Comprehension escaped me. "I don't get it. You observed me at my worst: bossing people around, making demands, being dominant to the point of belittling. I know how I can be. Dad always said I would have made a tough captain if I'd have followed in his footsteps. Why are you proud of that?"

"You said and did everything back there to honor Maggie."

A feeling of warmth passed over me, and I felt Maggie right there with us.

"Daddy, are you going to be the prince tomorrow?" Lily asked, bouncing up and down with energy Manda never remembered having.

"No, I'm sure your Auntie Manda will hire a professional for that job." Pete bent over and scooped her into his arms. "I'm a professional Daddy. And we have to ask Mommy about tomorrow."

"So can we go, Daddy? Can we?" Her eyes sparkled like a kid seeing the Fourth of July fireworks for the first time. "Maggie's books are my favorite!"

"Well, I told you. It depends on—"

I stomped my foot and crossed my arms. "I'm not taking

no for an answer. If it weren't for Lily, I never would have signed Maggie. Her second opinion is part of why this book is a huge success. Please, Pete?" I laced my fingers together with Lily's. We blinked at him with wide eyes.

"How can I say no?"

Lily squeezed Pete tightly. "Thank you. Thank you. Thank you!"

CHAPTER TWENTY-SIX

HARRY

"Love is a smoke raised with the fume of sighs"
(Romeo and Juliet 1.1.188)

More insistent knocking. Dane was sleeping, so I heaved myself out of my comfy computer chair and looked through the peephole. It was Manda!

This was my chance to explain. Introduce her to Dane and the whole messed up thing. Come clean about everything. I unlocked the door, and there she was. My stupid gut twisted up in knots, and my chest got tight. She was beautiful. "Hey."

"Hi. Look, I came to say I'm sorry about what happened with Pete." Heaps of guilt were piled around her, yet none of this was her fault.

"Harry, I think you have a split personality and need help. I actually came to ask you a favor, but now that I think about it, forget it." She spun and headed down the hall.

I followed her and caught her arm before she got too far. "You're right. I do." I was kind of excited to have her see Dane and me side by side in the flesh. "I'm getting the help I need. I swear. I have a therapist and everything. What's the favor?"

Manda was so damn cute. "I really...need..." she stammered.

The sparkle of intelligence in her eyes and the cloak of sincerity and kindness made me want to grab her, hold her tight, and never let go. "Go on," I motioned with a roll of my hand.

"I have a book signing tomorrow for Maggie's book. And no author. I don't know what to do besides buy an old prom dress and put on a tiara. I need Wolverine Romeo. I thought about calling the Shakespeare Theater to hire an actor, but I figured you'd be the one they'd send anyway." She laughed. "So I thought I'd skip the aggravation and ask you myself. It's only for a few hours, to charm little girls. Then I promise I'll be out of your life. Forever. Roger is taking over as your agent."

I blinked. Was she giving me another chance? "I'll be there."

"Thank you." Her phone piped up.

"Wait, I need to tell you something. Come back to my place. Meet my—"

Brother.

But she waved over her shoulder and began a conversation on her phone. "Manda Wolfgram. Yes, that is what I ordered. What do you mean not enough time?"

Desdemona barked. Dane poked his head out the door right as the stairwell door closed behind Manda. I grabbed his arm. "Come with me. I have to introduce you."

Dane followed me up the stairs, and we knocked on her door. My heart thumped in my chest. Finally! I knocked again. Beefer barked.

Shit. When she left, she hadn't gone up the stairs. She'd gone down. We missed her.

Back at our place, Dane padded into the living room,

cracked a beer, and plunked down on the couch after clearing a small section. Desdemona whined for a while before circling the usual three times and finally sighing and curling into a ball at his feet.

"So now what, Einstein?"

"Manda needs Romeo to make an appearance tomorrow morning at a book signing. Let's make sure she gets him. Can you snag an outfit for me to borrow from the theater?" I had a flash of brilliance on how I could make this right. At least with Manda.

Beer sloshed out of the bottle as Dane shot up to a standing position. "You got it. I'll make some calls and head over there right now. I think this is a great idea, Harry. Tell her the truth. All of it. She'll understand. I promise." He returned fully dressed and with his coat on. "Did you ever hear anything on that great tip you were supposed to get?"

"No," I lied. His life was more important than mine. And Manda seeing the truth would at least help her have some closure on the "us" that was never meant to be.

"Before I go, I'm going to ask one serious question. You know why I only go on two dates with women?"

I rolled my eyes. "Serious is the Sunday repertoire. Thursdays are set aside solely for sarcasm. Maniacal Mondays…" I ticked it off with my fingers. "Tethering Tuesdays. Serious is reserved for Sundays only."

"Harry!" Dane slammed his hand down on the arm of the coffee table. "I only go on two dates with most girls because of you."

"Yeah, because of me, the colossal embarrassment. I've ruined your life, too. Put another mark on the chalkboard." I was insulted. "I tried for a long time to end this for us. To find a way to protect women. You know every time we hired a girl and brought her back upstairs, I always slipped her a few hundred or, if she talked a good talk, a few grand. 'Get off the street,' I begged them. 'Move away from here. Start over.'"

Rubbing his temples, Dane nodded. "I know. But they never fail to disappoint us, do they? Cry. Thank us for the money. Promise to turn their lives around. And then…where do I see them in a few weeks? Back up to their old games. I'm to the point where I think our good intentions have been only that and nothing more. We are no closer to helping anyone. Psychopaths kidnap little girls and torture them for fun. And the two of us pretending to be vigilantes out for justice to find the bad guys, kick their asses, and save other little girls. That should be your version of the great American novel." Dane paced the floor. Obviously this whole speech had been building up inside him for a while. "I feel desensitized to it all. Look, I can't even pinpoint the day I stopped trying to help them. The day I gave up and submitted to what they wanted—cheap thrills and money. No frills sex for payment. And all the other girls I date don't ask for money, just everything else money can buy. I need to get out of here." Dane slammed down his beer. "Shit, when *did* I lose it?"

I hated watching Dane go down the rabbit hole. It was time to finish this. Let him move on. "Pack. Drive up to Wisconsin. Audition for that role. I'm heading up to Canada to find a quiet cabin to fish and write…what did you call it? The great American novel."

My brother's eyes lit up. "Seriously?"

"Yup, we'll split up the money and each go find a way to finally live." My thoughts drifted back to that hug from Manda. That pride in my work. The punch in the face from Pastor Pete. It had triggered something deep in the recesses of my heart. A promise to a little girl to be better. My sister would have wanted me to be better than this.

"She wouldn't want this for us, Harry."

"Who?"

"Our sister, Bro. We have to ditch this life and let her rest."

Tomorrow. Maybe I'd even be resting right next to her.

"I agree." We shook hands, and Dane left for the theater. I could see the burden lift from his shoulders. All our money would be in a box on Dane's bed before I left the house tomorrow morning. He alone would have the ability to move on, blame me for all the failures. I wanted Dane to move forward with his life.

CHAPTER TWENTY-SEVEN

MANDA

"Make way there for the princess!"
(King Henry the Eighth 5.3.63)

Monday morning

Strapless silk and poufy taffeta pink prom dress?
Check.
Tiara?
Check.
Sensible heels because kids won't look at my feet?
Check.

A few hours of tossing and turning were all that fueled me at the moment.

After today, I could sort out the Harry thing. Maybe we could be civil to each other. Maybe even friends. But that was a long shot. And only *if* he held true to his word and showed up to play the prince. It all depended on that.

Who knew? Maybe this would shape up to be a pretty good day.

I grabbed my computer bag, pat Beefer on the head, and locked the door behind me.

Peeking down the hallway, I wondered what the neighbors would think of the prom dress and sensible shoes. Thankfully, there was no one in the hallway or elevator to ogle my odd early-morning attire. It wasn't every day I pranced through the lobby dressed up like a princess. I held my head up high. *This is for you, Maggie!*

Planted without fail in his usual spot in the lobby stood George. A broom in hand, helping to keep his immaculate foyer in pristine condition.

"Hi, George." I waved.

He nodded and smiled. "Miss Wolfgram."

Not a raised eyebrow. Not a double take. Nothing.

The epitome of a professional.

"I'm a princess today, George. What do you think?" I twirled, and the dress rose in a circle around me.

"I say, 'May I have this dance?'" He bowed and held out his hand.

Setting down my belongings, I couldn't help it. George placed one hand on my waist and held my hand. With the timing and grace of a practiced dancer, George waltzed me around the couches, humming a few bars from *Swan Lake* in my ear. I lost myself in the glee of the moment, doing my best to follow George's masterful lead and not step on his toes. He held me at arm's length, brought me close, and even twirled me around. I felt an odd, unwelcome breeze over my torso as the revolving doors opened.

It was a real-life Prince Charming all decked out in Shakespearean regalia. Wolverine Romeo complete with sideburns this time. He stopped dead in his tracks, like a cartoon character who leans back on their heels and squeals to a stop.

"Manda!"

I registered the shock in his eyes. Looking down, I realized why. The strapless part of the dress was beneath my breasts, which were now on display for the masses, and right now, that happened to be Harry.

"Uh, George."

The doorman never missed a step. He swung me back close, covered me up, and gave me a gentle dip before he released me. "Thanks for the dance, Lady Manda."

"But the dress!" I sputtered. "I…"

"Well played, George." Harry clapped his hands. "Double-sided tape," he whispered in my ear. "You should look into it."

He helped with my things, and I practically ran out the front door. "Hold up!" he said, and I stopped. "You forgot this…for good luck."

He placed me against the nearest solid object, which happened to be the brick next to the revolving door of our building, and put his lips on mine. I was shell-shocked from the boob exposure incident and let it happen. No, I couldn't lie to myself. I wanted it to happen. My whole body lit up with sparks. He tasted like vanilla beans and pure Harry. The Harry part was way more delicious. I opened my eyes, looking around like PDA was a felony.

He rubbed my cheek with his thumb. "Starting to like me again, aren't you?" His eyes twinkled.

Then his jacket was pulled from behind. "Hey, what the heck?" Harry's fists clenched before he turned around.

"Seriously, Sis, do I have to hit this guy every time I see him? Or are you two finally getting along?"

"Pete, don't." I stepped between them before I realized Pete was joking.

"Hey man, good to see you." Pete stuck out his hand, and Harry shook it.

"Auntie Manda! Auntie Manda!" Lily wore an adorable pink polka dot party dress and a tiara. She bull-rushed her way straight into my arms for a bear hug. "You look beautiful!"

"Not as pretty as you, Lily. Look, you even wore the sparkly silver shoes I bought you!" I kissed her forehead. "How is my favorite niece?"

"I'm your only niece, Auntie Manda!" The girl waggled a finger in my face while correcting me. "Who's that? Your boyfriend? I saw you guys kissing and stuff!"

"Lily, you get smarter every time I see you! This is my friend, Harry."

"Nice to meet you." He shook her tiny hand, and she giggled.

"Hi, Sarah," I said. "Long time no see. Thanks for coming." I immediately saw the change between her and Pete. She was even holding his hand and giving him warm looks. Maybe she'd finally forgiven him even though she looked like she hadn't slept in a week.

My dad was only a few steps behind her. "Princess!" Dad held two steaming cups of coffee, giving me the best hug he could without dropping the beverages. "I'm glad to see you're getting your money's worth from that expensive prom dress. Remember how your mom tricked me into letting you have it, saying you could wear it to a few dances?"

"I do," I said. "She told you that even though it cost hundreds of dollars, I could wear it to at least four dances so it was like saving money. And you fell for it."

"And how many times did you wear it?" He kissed my cheek and took a sip of his coffee.

"It's definitely only a three-hundred-dollar dress now. And in less than ten years!"

"Harry, this is my father. Dad…Harry." They shook hands.

Everyone was ready. I choked back all the emotion that welled up in me having all these people come to support me. And Maggie.

NOT FOR ME

Once again, I found myself in a cab with Romeo. The others were behind us, and we all got let out by a side entrance of the bookstore where the bun lady and a few of her minions were ready to pounce. "Don't forget," Harry said, seeing that I was welling up. "Maggie is here in spirit. And I'll bet your mom is, too. They'd both be so proud of you. You got this, and I'll be right next to you the whole time. I promise."

"It means a lot that you showed up. But don't think that the kiss changes anything."

"Everything has changed, and you know it. But for now, just boss me around when we get there and tell me how to help."

Thirty minutes until the store opened. Trying my best to forget the mind-blowing kiss, I went into work mode. Like a cop directing traffic, I had one employee organizing books on the table, Harry on the banners, and my dad and Lily organizing the swag. Too bad that cupcake recipe was a bust. The bun lady's voice was getting shriller by the moment, and after an employee whispered something in her ear, she threw her hands in the air and marched up to me. I could almost see the steam coming out of the woman's ears.

"What's wrong, Pat?" I did my best to flutter my eyelashes and prepare for a reprimand of some kind.

"What's wrong?" Bun Lady was nearing hysterics. "Everything! The whole city of Chicago is on their way here!"

"What are you talking about?"

The bun lady pointed to the employee that had whispered in her ear. The woman held out her phone and played a voice message on speaker. I could see the lines of people forming outside. The line was already going around the corner. "Hello, students! This is Alan Peters, the superintendent of the Chicago school district. I wanted to call each of my elementary students personally and tell them about an exciting event today at the State Street Bookstore downtown during your holiday break. The latest book in the *Pink Cupcake Princess* series is being signed by the princess herself, and there will be free cupcakes! I am a huge fan of this series, and if you are looking for something fun to do with your kids, why not head down there? If you mention this call, the bookstore will give you a ten percent discount on any purchases in the store compliments of a local Chicago author. So, if your family has a chance, don't miss this event at 9:00 a.m. tomorrow morning."

The employee put down her phone, and everyone stared at me in silence like I had superpowers with connections. "I have a second grader," she stammered. "How the heck did you get him to do *that*?"

As Harry was working around me, he whispered in my ear. "Alan is a big fan of mine. I called in a favor. I hope you don't mind."

A huge crowd of parents and little girls milled around outside the store, spilling into the street. My heart sank and sang at the same time. Mean Bun Lady rushed over to me. "Who is paying for this discount?" she fumed.

Harry pulled out his credit card. "I am. Now please, show some respect to the princess."

Turning on her heel, she began barking orders at her staff.

"What can we do to help, Sis?" Pete laughed and clapped Harry on the back. "Nice one, by the way."

"Pete, can you fix that banner?" I pointed to a crooked one. "Lily, can you sprinkle this confetti everywhere?" Lily giggled and began throwing the sparkly confetti stuff, much to the chagrin of Bun Lady, whose left eye was beginning to twitch as she made her way to the front door.

"Sarah, can you make sure every little girl gets a tiara and a wand, a sprinkling of glitter, a free bookmark, a "Cupcake Princess" keychain, a magnet, and…?"

"And a cupcake, right?" Ally and Vanessa appeared out of

nowhere with a cartful of perfect pink cupcakes. Vanessa laughed. "You are a dumb blonde. When I asked you at Ally's for the baking soda, you gave me baking *powder*! Try them now. They are amazing!"

I took a nibble, and the cake and frosting melted in my mouth. "Wow!"

"We pulled an all-nighter baking. But look at all the people. I hope we have enough!" Ally pointed outside to the crowd. Kids were now pressing their noses against the window, and parents were starting to knock on the door.

I was as ready as I'd ever be.

Frantic employees ran around in circles. Books were stacked, cupcakes were organized, and a makeshift cash register was set out.

Mean bun lady gave me an apologetic nod and a weak smile before opening the door.

"The line goes around the corner! Great job, Manda!" Dad gave me a quick squeeze before I took my place.

I stared at Maggie's book. "This is for you, Maggie." For my favorite and most deserving author who would never enjoy the success of her books. For the series that Harry, who stood by my side, would allow to live on.

My brother held Sarah's hand, and Lily jumped around in circles and laughed like this was the best day of her life.

I let my emotions well up. Some moments were not meant to be snapped on camera but in the mind's eye.

This is one of those moments.

A redheaded, freckle-faced girl stepped forward, pushing the book toward me. She licked at the cupcake's pink frosting and made a yummy sound.

"Good morning. I'm Princess Manda. Can I sign this for you?"

CHAPTER TWENTY-EIGHT

HARRY

*"The world is grown so bad,
That wrens may prey where eagles dare not perch:"
(King Richard the Third 1.3.71)*

That kiss. Her lips.
If it was a prince she wanted, it was a prince she would get to the end.

If these were my last few hours on earth, I wanted to spend them with someone I loved.

And I love Manda.

It was my turn to be proud of Manda. Lines of people. Manda in her taffeta dress and a genuine smile on her face as she spoke with each family. My sister would have loved all this. I hoped wherever she was, she was at peace.

Pastor Pete's daughter, Lily, reminded me of my little sister. A ball of energy, flitting everywhere and trying so hard to help everyone.

I twirled each little girl in a circle, and Manda sprinkled them with glitter before signing their book. They each got a sparkly tiara and a cupcake. The smell of sugar and new hard cover books peppered the air as crisp pages were flipped for the first time. The din of families. The laughter of each little girl, excited to be out with her family and friends in the city. Each girl underwent a magical transformation when they reached Manda, like a brief vision that dreams can come true and life can have a happily ever after.

When it was over, I stepped to the side and snagged one of the cupcakes Vanessa and Ally had made. I sunk my teeth into the overpowering layer of frosting, letting my taste buds tingle with the joy of the sweetness. It was then I saw him.

Vito.

I knew that look. A predator, idly browsing a magazine and flipping pages, pretending to skim them without reading a word.

He watched the little *girls* still milling around the bookstore with their parents.

The hair on the back of my neck stood up. I edged my way back to Manda, who was starting to pack up, never taking my eye off of him. I reached for my phone and slipped it in a pocket.

By the time I looked for him again, he was gone. I exhaled a sigh of relief. He wouldn't be so stupid as to snatch a girl in public like this, would he?

Then behind the crowd that was beginning to leave, I saw him once again. Outside and out of my reach. Vito was holding the hand of a little girl with sparkly shoes. He shoved her in the back of a black sedan.

Vito chose the one little girl who didn't seem to belong to a family. The one little girl who was not attached to her mother's hip because her mother was busy doing something else.

Lily.

Pete and his wife were busy collecting bookmarks, tiaras, and wands. They weren't even watching Lily.

I grabbed Manda by the hand and yanked her outside. "We have to go." No fucking way was something going to happen on my watch. Not again. "Your niece just got kidnapped. I saw it."

"What?" Manda cried. "Are you sure?"

There was no time to waste. I yanked on her arm, half dragging her to the middle of the road where I flagged down a taxi.

The driver leaned out his window. "Where to?"

Ignoring him, I shoved Manda in and dove into the back of the cab. "Follow that black car. Now!" I said, waving a crisp hundred-dollar bill between the plexiglass that separated us. The man slid open the window and nabbed the currency before nodding and hitting the gas.

I leaned forward. "Left! They turned left."

"Got it," the cabbie said. Clearly in the biz for many moons, the cabbie asked no questions and kept pace with the black sedan without being too obvious. This definitely wasn't his first go-around being asked to follow someone.

"I need to call my dad." Manda hit "speaker." He picked up on the second ring.

"Dad, this is Manda. Where's Lily?"

"She must be with—say Pete, where's Lily?"

Pete's voice came from a distance away. "I don't know. Probably with Sarah. There she is."

I couldn't relax. I knew it was Lily with Vito. I was sure of it. But maybe…

"Where's Lily?" Sarah's voice escalated. "I thought she was with you, Pete!"

I couldn't hold my tongue and watch the sedan. "Sir, this is Harry. Your granddaughter was abducted by a man named Vito. They are in a black sedan headed south. We are in a cab in pursuit."

"License plate?"

"I can't make it out, sir."

Manda strained to look as well but shook her head. "We can't read it."

"I'll have the whole damn city following you as soon as I can."

Manda squeezed my hand. "I'm scared."

Without hesitation, Colonel Wolfgram's voice came through loud and clear through her speakerphone. "Remember, you are from a family who is at their best when things are at their worst. Don't lose that car, Harry."

"No, sir. Not on my watch." We hung up.

Our pace slowed to a crawl, and the world outside threatened to assault me. Screaming traffic, droves of humans, and the stench of garbage made me want to shout.

"Where are they?" Manda scanned the bumper-to-bumper traffic.

"There!" I pointed at the car. Then I saw it. The black sedan turned left, heading east toward an industrial section of long abandoned buildings on the wharf. "Hey, where are we?" I asked the cabbie.

"The old shipyard," the cabbie said. "But this area isn't used as much anymore since they built Navy Pier. Mostly industrial ships coming and going. Not the best neighborhood, if you catch my drift."

The taxi started looking out of place. If Vito knew he was being followed, we might never get Lily back. "Act like you got mixed up, and do a U-turn at the bottom of the hill," I instructed.

Complying without hesitation or question, the cabbie put on a blinker and waited. The sedan pulled up to a building with broken windows, and a long garage door was pulled open from the inside to admit the vehicle.

"Now what?" the cabbie asked.

I had already tapped out 911 on my phone to my contact,

but we needed to ditch this cab and get closer to the building. "Take her back." I stayed low and got out of the cab. "I'm going in."

"Not without me." She hopped out of the cab. I couldn't stop her, but this was no place for her. We made our way to the building until I stopped us, crouching down about thirty yards away from an entrance. I had to assess the situation. Adrenaline coursed through me, giving my senses a shot of extra power. "I need to get inside. You stay here. Call your dad and tell him where we are and promise me you won't move."

She nodded, and I gave her a quick kiss. The look in her eyes reflected her fear.

"I'll get her back. I promise."

My senses stayed on high alert as I picked my way closer to the building, working around the massive broken-down structure…only to come upon a nightmare.

I spied a viable cargo ship, small enough to be run by a small crew but large enough to get through the Saint Lawrence Seaway and cross the ocean that stood before them. But that wasn't the worst part. It was the words spoken by the two men outside.

"I was able to get one more. That makes ten." It was Vito.

"Are you ready to depart?" The other man must be the one they called "The Giant." A big guy who peeled off money that Vito slipped into his pocket. Lily's cash value. I had to hold myself back from rushing him right then and there.

"Give my crew five minutes," the other replied. "Then bring the girls out, blindfolded and tied tightly."

Five minutes? No time.

Slinking around the front of the building, I tried a rusty service door.

Unlocked. These guys had no reason to expect company down here. This whole area was pretty much dead and abandoned. A great place to stow little girls until they could be... shipped off to God knows where.

Fuck.

I heard noises and picked my way toward the sounds. Muffled moans from nine little girls and Lily.

"Ouch!" she said when a man shoved her forward. Another guy backhanded her hard, kicked her to the floor, bound her hands behind her back, and stuffed a dirty rag into her mouth.

"Move and you're dead, little girl."

My mind slowed to a crawl. Pushing down my pent-up venom, which threatened to overtake me, I promised my nervous alter ego I'd give it plenty of therapy later, but right now, I was kind of busy.

With one deep breath, I formulated a plan. Both men were packing handguns tucked into the back of their pants. I edged closer.

The whole world became crystal clear. Almost like an out-of-body experience. Every possible scenario of what might happen rapid-fired through my brain, and I knew what I had to do.

"Get them up," The Giant, in the suit, barked to the other guy leaning against the wall.

Reaching forward, I slipped the gun from the back of one of the guy's pants. He never even flinched. "Drop your weapon, and release the girls."

The Giant reached for his weapon. Instinct had already positioned my trigger finger in place, and necessity made my finger jerk toward me. I hit him square in the chest. The guy dropped.

"Shit." The other man drew his weapon, but I had already turned it on him and pulled the trigger a second time—my aim just as deadly.

"FBI! Hands in the air!"

I put up my hands. "I know. Who do you think called you?

Don't shoot me." I spun around slowly to see a plain-clothed guy with a gun trained on my chest.

Vito and the other hired hand came rushing in from the docks, weapons drawn. The Fed shot the first guy but paused when he saw Vito. "You?"

"Hey, Jonah. Long time no see."

I backed away, out of firing range.

"I heard you went rogue. Undercover life finally pull you in?"

"I'm so deep undercover even bedbugs don't know I'm there."

"This bedbug does." *Bang*!

And that was the end of Vito.

"So you're the infamous Harry Sackes?" The FBI guy went from body to body, checking each for a pulse.

"Yeah. What about Vito's girl...the one I was supposed to meet at 11:30?"

"Safe."

I rushed over to Lily, whose eyes were pressed closed. "You're safe now." I untied her hands and feet and removed the rag from her mouth.

She dove into my arms. "Thank you! I told Auntie Manda you were a real prince!"

"That one yours?" Jonah asked.

I nodded.

"Well, Agent Romeo, I already called this in, so you know what happens next." He picked up the gun I had fired and wiped it clean before laying it next to Vito. "You better split. Don't go too far," he said with a knowing wink.

"I'm out. Don't call me again. I won't answer." I grabbed Lily's hand and tugged her outside to find Manda when we heard the sirens. Lily ran to Manda, and they hugged each other tightly. Our cabbie had stayed in the same spot, his left turn signal still blinking. I helped Lily and Manda into the car and pulled the door shut behind us.

"We can go?" Manda asked.

I gave the cabbie our address, and when we hit the main road, six police cars, sirens blowing, headed toward the warehouse. I'd explain everything to Manda later. Right now, we needed to get as far away from this place as we could.

Lily clung to us both.

I threw more money in the front seat. "Thanks for waiting. You did good, man."

I turned to face forward.

Life was too short to look back.

CHAPTER TWENTY-NINE

MANDA

"Love looks not with the eyes, but with the mind;"
(A Midsummer Night's Dream 1.1.234)

In the midst of the worst day of my life, save losing my mother, a piece of truth slid into place when Harry and I walked into the lobby and there was another Romeo standing there.

"Manda, this is the real Dane Sackes. My twin, the actor."

"Twin?" I asked, bewildered, all the pieces falling into place.

"Sorry I missed the whole book party thing," Dane said, "but guess what? I got a call to audition for Puck at that outdoor theater in Wisconsin next week!"

Harry gave him a congratulatory pat on the back when I realized Lily looked even more confused than I did.

"There are two of you?" I asked.

The elevator opened, and people rushed to meet us. When Lily saw her parents, she released her death grip on Harry and dove into their arms.

"Lily!" Sarah and Pete formed a triad of hugs, kisses, and tears.

My dad was there. And Vanessa. Even Ally. They all mobbed Lily, asking her if she was okay and what had happened. I noticed Harry pull Dane aside and talk to him.

Vanessa was the first to notice Dane and Harry. "Whoa." I knew she saw a carbon copy of Harry in Dane. "Harry?" she asked Dane.

"I'm Dane. That's Harry, my better half. I believe your friend has fallen madly in love with him. It was me you hung out with at the bar." He winked at her.

"But..." She pointed back and forth between them. "I don't understand."

Lily broke free from her parents' and went back to hugging Harry. "You're silly, Vanessa. This is Romeo, my hero. He beat up the bad guys and saved me. And that's his twin brother, Dane. Can't you tell by the nose?"

I saw it now. Side by side, there were subtle differences.

Harry ripped off his fake sideburns, exposing his scar. "As Shakespeare said, 'Truth makes all things plain.'"

I put my arm around him.

A broad smile came over his face, and he wrapped his arm around the back of my dress.

Pete looked to his wife. "Well then, I might as well come clean. The congregation voted me out. I have no job, no house, and I'd have to check with Sarah on how much money we have left."

She dropped her head. "We have two thousand in savings, honey."

With a jerk, Pete turned on her. "What? We have much more than that. I know we do."

Her legs wobbly, Sarah opened her purse and pulled out a long document that she handed to Pete. "I made up my mind after the church vote. I was going to tell you today after your sister's release party. I bought us a small cabin on a trout stream in Alaska. It needs some work, but I figured the three of us could go up, reconnect, and find each other again."

Pete broke down. She'd forgiven him and obviously believed in him. Enough to dump their life savings into his dream and make a new life.

At that moment, I realized I'd do the same thing for Harry. Whatever it took, I'd always stand by his side. *Love alters not when it alteration finds*.

Dad came forward and clapped Harry on the back. "I heard from a little birdie you saved a lot of lives today, young man."

"Holy shit man, you did it!" Dane's voice was creepy to me now, because it was hard to tell them apart unless I looked at them. "Harry, maybe everything that's happened to us led to today. I mean, everything. I feel like a tremendous weight is lifted, like Julie finally forgives us for not being there to help her."

Harry looked away and brushed at his face. "Yeah, I feel it, too."

"I never blamed you, Harry. It was never your fault. But today, you are definitely the hero, Bro."

I hugged them both. "It feels kind of funny to be holding two Sackes."

CHAPTER THIRTY

HARRY

"I to the world am like a drop of water,
That in the ocean seeks another drop;"
(The Comedy of Error 1.2.35-36)

Manda's door was unlocked. I went inside. Holy mercy the woman was sexy, barefoot in a prom dress, her blonde locks falling in wisps around her face. "I want to scoop you up and put you on the top of an ice cream cone."

"Hi, you." Her voice was an invitation.

My breathing was ragged. "You met the real me on our first date. You make me fearless." I easily picked her up and carried her to the bedroom. I saw the panic in her eyes. "No, the dogs don't need to go out. Yes, I shut and locked the front door. No, I don't care that your pink comforter has dog hair all over it. Relax." I placed her on the bed, staring at her with a hunger to please I'd never known. I spoke the first words that came to my mind as I undressed her…slowly.

Let me not to the marriage of true minds

Admit impediments. Love is not love
Which alters when it alteration finds,
Or bends with the remover to remove:
O no! it is an ever-fixed mark,
That looks on tempests and is never shaken,
It is the star to every wandering bark,
Whose worth's unknown, although his height be taken.
Love's not Time's fool, though rosy lips and cheeks
Within his bending sickle's compass come;
Love alters not with his brief hours and weeks,
But bears it out even to the edge of doom.
If this be error, and upon me proved,
I never writ, nor no man ever loved.

I'd fallen in love with this woman. "I'm sorry I'm not normal."

"Normal is boring," she said in a breathy voice. "What will you write now?"

I extracted something very tangled from her hair, producing the crooked tiara. "Whatever you want me to write, my princess. How about tonight, you wear this?" I pointed to the tiara. "Only this."

She reset the tiara and gave me a playful punch on the arm. "I don't act like a princess."

I trickled kisses down her neck. She closed her eyes and melted into me, yielding to my touch. "No more talking." I gave her soft kisses at first, testing her lips. I forgot her bedroom, forgot our surroundings, yielding more to her receptive touch.

My insides rumbled with a need for her coursing through me. And I loved it.

From my tingling toes to the fiery crackle roaring between my legs, to my heart pounding in time with hers, I lost track of all things earthly. I heard music where there was none. I saw colors in the room that weren't there. All my senses were on overload, and this one woman, this one moment encompassed my every thought, emotion, feeling, and physical sensation.

All else forgotten.

Only the heat of our bodies vying to get as close as possible. We locked eyes. Manda became the only thing in the universe that I cared about and would ever get my attention again.

∽

She dozed on my shoulder, both of us falling in and out of blissful sleep. I had to ask. "I'll bet you wanted candles, music, rosebuds, the cover of darkness. A prince."

"I thought I did."

My insides ached again at the sound of her voice. "I vow, from this point on, to only give you what you want." I crawled off the bed and knelt in front of her. "You can wear whatever you want, take me wherever you want, but please know the *you* I fell for is this you. Sweatpants and glasses. Having wine and cheese on your couch. I'll be a prince. But I'll only be a prince for one princess…you. I love you, Manda Wolfgram. In fact, you're more than a princess, and I'll only ever treat you as my queen."

ABOUT THE AUTHOR

Kat was born and raised in Milwaukee, Wisconsin where she learned to roller skate, ride a banana seat bike, and love Shakespeare. She holds a Doctor of Pharmacy degree and is happily employed as a retail pharmacist. She is married to her soul mate, composer Lee de Falla and raising four kids together ala the Brady Bunch. She is afraid of heights and outright panics if there no creamer for morning coffee.

Register for her newsletter to learn about her upcoming projects and find out about deals and giveaways at http://eepurl.com/MFZ55

- facebook.com/authorkatdefalla
- twitter.com/@katdefalla
- instagram.com/katdefalla
- goodreads.com/AuthorKatdeFalla
- bookbub.com/profile/kat-de-falla

ALSO BY KAT DE FALLA:

The 7 Archangels Series is the Black Dagger Brotherhood by J.R. Ward meets The Da Vinci Code by Dan Brown. Fans of dark fantasy and non-stop action will love this series!

DARK FANTASY (The 7 Archangels Series)

The Seer's Lover

Darkwalker

Moto Maddie's BMX Portal is great for kids 8 and up who love Goosebumps books by R.L. Stine or My Big Fat Zombie Goldfish. The books are a mash-up of The Goonies meets The Sand Lot. Kat began this series when her four kids told her there was nothing "good" to read so she asked them for ideas and ba-da-bing...Flying Mutant Zombie Rats was born!

MIDDLE GRADE FANTASY (Moto Maddie BMX Portal Series)

Flying Mutant Zombie Rats

Slime-Spewing Vampire Velociraptors

Kat also co-writes the Haunts for Sale Series as Kat Green. This series follows Sloane Osborne - paranormal real estate agents. Fans of Ghost Adventures and The Dead Files will devour this fast-paced series. Find out more at: www.hauntsforsale.com

PARANORMAL SUSPENSE (Haunts for Sale Series writing as KAT GREEN)

First Contact

Second Sight

ACKNOWLEDGMENTS

Thanks to Kelly Hashway my relentless editor who makes my stories shine.
And a shout out to my beta readers extraordinaire Rachel and Heidi for convincing me I'm sometimes funny out loud and for real, not just in my own head.

Made in the USA
Columbia, SC
15 April 2019